THE
DARK
UNDERWORLD

THE CHOSEN COVEN
BOOK TWO

To Rylanne,

D. L. BLADE

Social Media:
Instagram: booksbydlblade
Facebook: dlblade
Twitter: DLBlade_Writer

Editing by Christina Kaye www.xtinakayebooks.com
Formatted by Affordable formatting
Book design by Redbird Designs
Proofreader: Rose Lawton www.instagram.com/rose.proof

Printed and bound in the United States of America.
First printing edition May, 2019.

Published by Fifth Element Publishing
Author, D.L. Blade
www.dlbladebooks.com

The Chosen Coven Trilogy

Read in order:

The Dark Awakening
The Dark Underworld
The Dark Deliverance

This book is dedicated to my very supportive husband. He has been a rock throughout my journey in bringing this book to life.

CHAPTER ONE

Deep breath, Mercy. You've been in way worse situations than this. If you can relax, you'll be able to muster an idea of how to get out of this situation.

"Focus," I muttered to myself. "Just focus."

I sucked in a breath and slowly released it, hoping that would slow down my heart rate. Each breath I released burned my dry mouth. I assumed I'd been six feet under for at least two to three hours. I wasn't sure how long it would take for me to consume all the oxygen, but I couldn't imagine it being much longer than this. The air was thick, and it became harder to breathe with each minute that passed.

It's not like I could die in here. It would just really suck to be stuck in a wooden box for eternity.

I hadn't died and come back yet since I had become immortal. I wondered how that would play out. Would I pass out, open my eyes again, pass out, wake up, and repeat that over and over again until I lost my mind?

My muscles quivered just thinking about the two creeps who had put me down, but I also cursed myself for being so stupid. I should've been paying better attention to my surroundings.

It wasn't about getting out of this situation so I didn't suffer . . . it was about getting out so I could make *them* suffer.

Come on, guys. Where are you?

I looked around the wooden coffin they had forced me into after they'd injected me with God only knew what, which had crippled my powers. Once the drug had worn off, I'd opened my eyes to this nightmare—I had been buried alive.

I knew this was going to happen, eventually. It was the only way they knew of to stop me, as long as the dagger was hidden away from their grasp.

I currently had my palm open so I could use my powers to light up the walls around me.

Man, it's hot in here.

Sweat dripped down my forehead, and the taste of salt consumed my senses as it touched my lips and entered my mouth. I rubbed the sweat off my lips with my other hand and looked around the small and cramped space. The earth was slowly seeping through the cracks every time I shifted my body.

This wasn't one of those fancy, metal caskets stuffed with white cushion padding they use at most burials today. This was a tattered, wooden coffin that looked like it came straight out of the Stone Age. The wood had split in several places, and I feared the whole thing would crumble on top of me if I so much as sneezed.

I placed my hands on the top of the lid and applied some

pressure. When I pushed, even slightly, the wood cracked, causing the dirt to seep through again.

I couldn't use my powers; it would have only caused the ground above to crush me, then I'd die of suffocation over and over again for eternity.

Now, that would be worse than passing out.

I didn't have much time.

I watched the earth slowly fall through the crack near my chest, the dirt and small round pebbles hitting my chest.

That's it! I beamed.

Earth.

Ezra's element.

Without skipping a beat, the tip of my finger reached for the earth. I pressed my index finger deep into the soil through a small hole right above my chest. I focused on Ezra. He *was* the ground we walked on. He'd feel it.

"Ezra, I'm right here," I whispered quietly. "Where are you guys?"

My pulse pounded faster when I closed my eyes and brought myself into a state of meditation in order to focus on what I had needed to do to reach him.

This needs to work.

I kept my finger on the soil for what felt like hours, but time seemed to move differently in there, or the lack of oxygen messed with my head.

Oh, crap.

The coffin cracked, the dirt poured in, and I had to remove my finger to cover my face.

Panic rose in my throat. What had I done?

I felt a jolt but kept my hands hovering over my face. The coffin rattled, and the lid blasted high in the air like an explosion. I moved my hands to see the earth and wooden coffin parts swirling around the hole I had been in, as if I were in the eye of a tornado. I drew in a deep breath of fresh air and briefly closed my eyes while still in the center of the dust devil. When I opened my eyes again, I saw my coven standing around it, with Ezra's hands outstretched, his eyes glowing an ashy brown color.

He lowered his arms, releasing the earth, as I reached for the top of the hole I had been in. Caleb reached for me and pulled me out.

"Oh, thank goodness," he cried as he pulled me to his chest, holding me tightly.

All of the tension I had held in was finally released. "Thank you, guys. Thank you."

The lightheadedness dissipated as my powers healed the trauma my body had experienced while buried alive. Being immortal didn't make me invincible. I still felt pain just like any mortal would. I also felt fear and anger, sadness and hopelessness. Right now, I mostly felt anger. Heat flushed through my body as I looked around to see if the vampires were nearby.

The coven ran to me and pulled me into a group hug. "They're probably long gone by now," Simon said as he released our embrace. "Unless they're that stupid."

"They're that stupid," I said through gritted teeth as my

attention left Simon and focused on the two vampires who had stuck me inside the coffin running from the cottage next to us.

"Seriously, they buried you in their front yard?" Leah asked. She shook her head as the two idiots fled the scene.

I frowned at that thought. They had been here the entire time, knowing I was suffering right outside their own door.

Caleb gestured in their direction. "They're all yours, Mercy."

A smirk replaced my frown as I raised my hands, energy flowing through my fingertips, and pulled my hands forward, blasting my force in their direction. The force of my magic slammed into their backsides, sending them airborne. It only took a minute for the pair to stand on their feet again, facing us with fangs out and fire burning in their eyes. Caleb handed me my stake and I ran toward them. The vampires froze in place.

Once I reached them, they fell to their knees, pleading.

Oh, come on.

"Please don't kill me. I don't want to die," cried the one who had mocked me earlier as he grabbed my throat to toss me into the coffin. "Just turn us human," he pleaded.

I chuckled at his words. That was what I had offered them as they shoveled dirt over me for thirty minutes. I had given them an out. I had warned them my coven would find me and that they'd be hunted down until I stuck a stake through their hearts.

They hadn't listened.

The second one held up his hands in defeat. "Please, I have a wife and—"

Poof! He was dust.

Caleb stood there holding his own stake. The first one closed his eyes, but when he opened them again, they were red.

"You'll pay for that, bitch! And when you do, I'll make you all suffer," he threatened, flashing his sharp and deadly fangs.

I leaned down, placed the stake to his chest, and shook my head. "Have fun in hell, asshole."

My stake impaled his chest with a quick thrust, and I watched him turn to dust. He would now join his friend in whatever afterlife those creeps went to.

"Well, I'm ready for dinner," I stated, but felt my voice crack. "Actually, I could really use some water."

"Water, yes, but food will have to wait. Something happened on Main Street a couple hours ago. There are police everywhere," Caleb explained.

"East Greenwich?" I asked.

Caleb nodded.

"Vampire attack?"

Leah shrugged. "We don't know yet, but Lily told us someone died."

My stomach twisted into knots. Was this someone we knew?

"What time is it?" I asked Ezra, who stood next to me.

Ezra looked down at his phone. "Midnight. Lily told us it

happened around ten, just a few hours after you went missing."

Caleb reached into his pocket and pulled out my phone. I had dropped my purse when they attacked me. I didn't even have a moment to defend myself before the needle had pricked my neck.

I had planned on meeting the coven for a couple rounds of pool when they'd snatched me. We were right outside of downtown Providence. Not once since this all started had they attacked so close to our town. I hadn't expected it.

"Let's go, then," I ordered, and we hurried to Simon's car. As much as I didn't want the attack to be from a vampire, it was the only way we'd find the ones that had to go. The ones that refused to turn human. The ones like the two we had just killed.

They were worthless, evil, and undeserving of our mercy.

CHAPTER TWO

"What happened," I asked an officer, my eyes narrowing in on his badge, "Officer Shields?"

The officer was handsome, for a guy who looked to be around forty. His mustache was shaved thin and his hair was light brown with a few silver streaks along the sides of the head, right above the ears.

He leaned against a Victorian-style, steel light post next to Tippy's Pancake House, writing something on his little black notepad. Yellow caution tape had been wrapped around the post and it stretched all the way over to the other side of the parking lot.

He ignored me, of course. I was just a teenage looky-loo, and he most likely had orders to keep things quiet until they received the official report to release to the public. I glanced past him, but all I saw were a dozen or so cops inside, moving around and conversing with each other.

"Is Tippy okay?" I asked. "I mean . . . Ryan Harrison?" When he didn't respond, I kept prying. "Look, I live right down the street. I just want to make sure it isn't someone I know." He glanced in my direction, shook his head, and walked away. "Don't worry," I mumbled to myself. "We'll find out soon enough."

The thought of it being Ryan, or as we call him, "Tippy," made my heart sink. It was his restaurant, and it had happened around the time he would have been locking up.

Lily appeared from behind the building. "I asked a few detectives on the other side, but they aren't giving me any answers. You?"

I shook my head. My stomach was in knots again, thinking it could be someone we knew. Maybe even a close friend.

I turned my attention toward the parking lot to search for Caleb, who was trying to get answers, too, but when I shifted to the right, I bumped into him.

He crossed his arms over his chest and shook his head with a slight side smirk. "The Mercy I know wouldn't have given up so easily." He winked at me and sauntered toward Tippy's, crouching under the caution tape near the front entrance.

"What are you doing?" I uttered in a near whisper. "They won't let you in there." Caleb reached the doors as they opened with the backside of an officer, pulling the front of a gurney. Once they emerged from the doorway, I immediately eyed the black tarp over the shape of what I assumed was a body.

A year ago, a corpse would have made my skin crawl and I'd have cowered at the sight of it, but not anymore. This last year, we'd cleaned up or reported a few dead bodies, mostly between Boston and Salem. The unsettling feeling inside me wasn't caused by the fact someone had died in my city. It was caused by the thought it could be someone we knew.

But why here? And why now? The only time they had ever come here to East Greenwich was because of me. We'd made a treaty with them six months ago that I would leave them alone as long as they didn't kill a human or turn one against their will. I had even given them a choice before driving a stake through their chest. Well . . . most of the time.

The choice was simple—become human again or die. The ones that were just downright evil always chose death or tried to fight me before I ended it for them.

Vampires like Dorian were proof enough that there were good ones among the fold. It had just taken me a while to convince the rest of the coven. Most of the vampire clans listened and obeyed this new "law," but there were a few bad seeds. And those bad seeds were the ones that kept us fighting.

Caleb moved to the side and let the cops walk by, but Officer Shields spotted him as he exited Tippy's.

"Hey, get on the other side of the tape. Now!" Shields warned.

Caleb threw his hands in the air in defeat. "All right. All right."

"The Caleb I know wouldn't have given up so easy," I teased as he joined me back in the parking lot.

"No! Ryan!" a female voice shouted from my right. Caleb and I turned our attention toward Tippy's grandmother, Joanne, as she ran toward the restaurant. "No!" she screamed again, pressing her hands to her chest as if she were experiencing chest pain. Her legs gave out from under her, and her knees hit the pavement. An officer ran toward her to assist and give her aid.

Oh, no.

Her words shattered my heart. Tippy was my friend.

I turned back to Caleb and slowly wrapped my arms around his waist. The world seemed to slow down as I wiped a single tear rolling down my face, and a sudden coldness hit me at my core. I looked up at him. "Why?" I turned to look back at Joanne again, who was now trying to push past the officers lining the caution tape. "Why would anyone hurt Tippy?"

Joanne almost collapsed to the floor again, but the officer held on to her shoulders, keeping her on her feet.

He escorted Joanne over to a police car and sat her in the passenger's side, and she buried her face in her hands.

"Would a vampire really do this?" I asked Caleb while choking back a sob.

He shook his head. "We'll find out. Don't worry."

We knew we weren't going to get any answers tonight, so we headed home to sleep. However, sleep was impossible for me. It was four in the morning, and I still had Tippy and his poor, sweet grandma on my mind.

I browsed the news on my phone, and our local news

channel reported what they had learned from the scene so far. Tippy had been killed shortly after ten in the evening after he'd locked up the restaurant. A couple had come to eat there, didn't realize they were closed, and had seen him on the floor through the window, covered in blood.

Evidence showed that he was in the middle of mopping the floor when someone had broken in and taken his life. Someone had shattered the back window by a corner booth, and muddy footprints lined the walkway that led to where they'd found Tippy's body.

They didn't release any information on how he died, but Caleb would be following up with our medical examiner friend, who had been helping us this last year.

"We need to have a connection that allows us to determine if it's a human or a vampire attack," Caleb told me a year ago.

Brown University had asked Melissa to speak to the pre-med students in the spring, and though it was a bold move for us to fill her in on what we were, we had approached her after the seminar and shared with her a world she hadn't known existed. She, of course, freaked out at first, but she was also happy to know the truth.

We had to know if the victim was attacked by a vampire so we could be the ones to handle it. It would put the police force in danger if they were tracking a creature they didn't know how to take down.

I sent a text to Caleb, as I was sure he wasn't sleeping, either.

Me: *I'm coming with you tomorrow. Tippy was my friend. I want to be there for this one.*

Caleb: *I'll pick you up at ten. Try to rest. We had a long night.*

Me: *Night.*

I closed my phone and rolled over onto my side. Whoever hurt Tippy was going to pay. Whether it be behind bars or in a pile of ash.

CHAPTER THREE

C aleb and I reached the backdoor to the morgue, and we waited on the side brick wall for Melissa to inform us once she had the cameras down. Surveillance was on every corner of the morgue, and we couldn't risk Melissa getting in trouble for sneaking us in.

Melissa texted Caleb, telling him the cameras were down and that she was on her way to get us. Once the door cracked open, she waved us in and led us to the autopsy suite.

A cold snap hit me when we entered the suite and a shiver ran up my spine, so I wrapped my sweater around my waist. Melissa zipped open the yellow bag which held Tippy's body, and my heart sank when I saw his still and life-less face.

"Vampire," Melissa said. "See the bite marks?" She pointed to two red holes on the side of Tippy's neck.

I glanced up at Caleb and back to Melissa. "Drained to death?" I asked.

She shook her head. "No. I was at the scene last night taking photos. The amount of blood on the floor is about the same amount that was missing from the victim."

When I glanced up at Caleb, he looked as confused as me.

Melissa saw our expression and continued. "He didn't drink from the body, Mercy. His fangs pierced the carotid artery, and he bled to death on the floor. The vampire attack victims I've examined in the past were drained." She pointed to the bites again. "The vampire who did this did it to kill, not feed."

I caught my breath and stared at her, wide-eyed. Caleb must have seen my shock. He inched toward me, bringing his fingers to mine and lightly rubbing my palm to help me relax.

I didn't mind him touching me. I cared for him, and we were always going to be in each other's lives. He wasn't touching me in a romantic manner. He was showing me he cared. He knew Tippy was someone I knew, and even though I had to put on a brave face so I could focus on this murder case with my coven, it still hurt to learn he was dead.

Not just dead but slaughtered by a vampire.

I just couldn't understand why a vampire would randomly kill a human. Did Tippy know him? Were there more vampires in our town than we thought, or did someone go out of their way to come down here and take his life?

Vampires didn't attack like this unless there was a reason. They'd kill if someone betrayed them. They'd drink if they were hungry, but they never wasted the blood.

Maybe they had been interrupted by someone coming to the café and they couldn't finish?

"Thanks, Melissa," I said, pulling my focus back to the room.

She zipped up the bag and grabbed a notebook off a metal desk in the corner of the room. "My report will state that an ice axe was most likely the weapon. Manner of death: homicide. Cause of death: blood loss."

Caleb glanced at me then shook Melissa's hand as if he had just completed a business meeting. "Thank you."

I rolled my eyes, directing my attention away from them so they didn't see. They were being ridiculous. I wasn't blind. I knew they had been dating, but he was being so weird about sharing that with me.

"We'll be in touch," Caleb said, and turned back to me. "Let's go train."

Last year, after my mom died, I inherited everything she had, including what was already in my trust. I decided it was best to get my own place, so I didn't put Lily's life in danger within our "witches vs. vampire" crossfire. Yes, she had magic to protect herself, but even with her powers, this was too much for her to handle. I didn't want her involved and risking her life for me anymore, but also, she had someone in her life now who didn't know about us. That alone could put *him* in danger.

Lily had been dating Bradley since last December. He was handsome, but Bradley was the epitome of a stereotypical computer geek. He wore thick glasses, hair parted to one side, and if he wasn't wearing a Star Wars shirt or his favorite black shirt with yellow, vinyl lettering that read, "I'm Geeky and I Know It," he wore a white button-up short-sleeve with suspenders and a bow tie. I didn't judge his lack of fashion sense because he made her laugh, and that was what mattered to her and to me.

Caleb had helped me find a property in East Greenwich with the rest of the coven. He still had his cabin in Salem, but he and his father mostly slept at Abigail's mansion in her spare rooms. Her place was big enough, and once I turned Abigail and Desiree human again, they hadn't been back to the house. Being able to visit tropical locations and seeing a world in the daylight again was the only thing that mattered to them anymore.

Riley and Amber formed their own pack and resided in Providence so Riley could live in the dorms at Brown University. It didn't matter that he was a werewolf now. He was going to attend college. His roommate at Brown, Aaron, and his sister, Hannah, became werewolves shortly after their fall semester. Riley explained that no one had forced them into being werewolves, like he had been, but that they had chosen to be bitten.

Riley informed me at a coffee shop around January that he and Amber were dating, but that they kept the pack a priority. They'd assist us when we needed help tracking down a vampire clan. I, of course, hated getting him involved, but the other four in the coven felt we fought better with a wolf pack by our side.

Shannon moved up north to attend the University of

Connecticut. She had always planned to attend Brown with us, but it was too close to everything that happened last year.

I got it. I didn't want my friends involved in this life.

Ever.

Shannon was smart to pretend nothing supernatural was going on around her. We spoke a few times a week on the phone, but we kept the conversations brief, and she was careful not to ask questions that could lead to answers she didn't want to hear.

And then there was Cami . . .

CHAPTER FOUR

I entered Cami's room quietly and spotted her in the corner of her dark, gloomy bedroom, staring at a canvas painted with black swirls, mist-like, surrounding a grove of trees. "Oh, no. This is all wrong. It needs more black," she said. She gripped the paint brush next to her and glided the black paint around the edges, circling the brush to the center. "That's better." She turned around to face me. "Hi, Mercy." Her voice was flat and emotionless.

She had removed all the pastel colors that had covered the walls and furniture of her room the moment they'd released her from the hospital. "The bright colors are blinding me," she had told me.

"Hey, Cami." I stepped further into her room, scanning over the walls covered in paintings like the one she worked on now.

Always black.

Always depressing.

None of her paintings made sense. Black paint covered most of the canvas, usually surrounding a forest or a river. It was unsettling.

After Cami awoke from her "coma," she wasn't Cami

anymore. I know she must have seen disturbing images or felt something during her possession that forever changed her, and there wasn't a spell we could conjure to bring her back from that nightmare. I leaned down next to her and looked up at the painting. "It's beautiful. Can I have this one? It will look great in our training room."

She stared at her feet, avoiding eye contact with me as she nodded.

"I'll see you tomorrow, okay?" She looked up and grabbed my wrist as if she were trying to keep me from leaving. I grabbed her hand and pried her fingers from my wrist. "Caleb and I are going to train for the rest of the day with my coven, but I told him I wanted to stop by to see you. I'll be back. I promise."

I lowered her hand toward the paintbrush.

"Are you sleeping?" I asked her. She shook her head, keeping her eyes on her feet. "Okay." I pulled out two sleeping pills from my purse and placed them on her night-stand. I had been supplying them for her a few times a week because every spell we had tried wasn't working. I grabbed the painting on the easel and replaced the spot with a blank canvas for her. She grabbed the paintbrush and started over.

Back at my house, I entered the spacious basement where we had been training for the last year. Ezra and Simon shared a room in the far-left corner, sleeping on a bunkbed, like two college roommates, while we used the rest of the space.

We had lined the walls with steel hooks and racks we could hang our wooden stakes and silver daggers on, and in the center laid a two-inch-thick pad that stretched from one end of the room to the other. Ezra bought a boxing bag that we kept in the corner by the bathroom, and he and I were the only ones who ever really worked out with it.

Leah descended the stairs with her hair pulled up in a short ponytail, barefoot and wearing a tank top with yoga pants. She was tiny, especially without shoes, but she could do some damage when she fought.

"Was it a vampire or human?" she asked us.

"Vampire," Caleb said as I opened my mouth to answer her.

"More fun for us." Ezra beamed, coming over to the pad while he pounded his right fist into his palm.

"Ezra, be sensitive. Mercy knew him," Leah snapped.

"It's fine. He was a great guy, but we have to focus on our mission. Caleb is having Roland look into The Black Horse clan," I explained.

Leah nodded. "Those are good places to start. We've been waiting for that clan to start something."

The Black Horse had moved to Providence shortly after I went through my Awakening, but they'd agreed to stay out of our way. I hadn't met any of the vampires from the clan, but Roland had a friend, Marcus, who was part of their "family." Marcus never reported any mischief that went on within the clan. He promised us they had changed their questionable behavior after my Awakening, and they were trying to change the future of how vampires treated the humans and witches they came across. As much as I wanted to trust Marcus, I wasn't ready, yet.

The nightclub they built had broken ground this spring and had opened two weeks ago. Regardless of Marcus's reports, we still kept an eye on them, and we would especially pay closer attention to the clan now. Their reputation preceded them, and a nightclub would be the perfect hideaway in which to commit shady vampire crimes. It was dark, the windows hidden by shades to keep the vampires safe from the light, and entry to the underground level was by exclusive invitation only.

"We haven't had a body in months." I tossed up a hand. "Then this happens. It's perfect timing, don't you think?"

Simon appeared from the bedroom, carrying a bag in his hand, and tossed it on the floor. "Are we assuming they're after Mercy again, given that it happened a few minutes from us?"

"It is our hometown." I faced Caleb. "This looks like something someone may do to get to me. What do you think?"

Caleb was focused only on his phone.

"Caleb?" Leah called.

He looked up and sighed. "Probably, but we still need to investigate before we call them out and demand justice. We don't want to create a war. I'll check it out."

"Let me do it." The pitch of my voice went up a notch. "Sarah can come over tonight to help me. I just need to scope the place and leave. Once I see what we're up against, we can come up with a plan and discuss whether we should be focusing on them or somewhere else," I explained, but I could already see Caleb shaking his head. He hated when I went undercover without him. "We aren't making the same mistakes we did last year, Caleb. I can do this." His mouth formed a straight line and he flared his nostrils. "Stop looking at me like that."

He rolled his eyes. "I'd feel safer if I were there."

"No way. The last time we investigated inside a bar, a vampire hit on me, and you broke his nose."

His jaw muscles tightened. "He healed."

I huffed and shook my head as I knelt to unzip the bag Simon had tossed onto the floor, ignoring Caleb's bitter response. I grabbed five sets of hand wraps, tossed them over to everyone, and put on my own. "We're sparring today. Leah, I'll pair up with you. Caleb, you be the attacker this time. Ezra, you're the victim. Simon, you can help Leah if Caleb gets the upper hand."

"I'm always the victim," Ezra whined. "Let Simon be the bait, and I'll be the vampire."

"You scream like a little girl, Ezra. You're the perfect target," I teased.

Ezra stuck out his tongue, dragged his feet to the center of the mat, and laid down on his back. After a few more seconds of Ezra mumbling obscenities at us, he finally said,

"Oh, no. Is that a vampire?" His voice was flat, and he crunched his face at Caleb, who hovered over him.

Caleb pretended to show his fangs and dashed toward Ezra. Leah quickly leaped in his direction and pounced on his back like a tiger attacking her prey. She wrapped her arm around his neck and her legs around his waist. They struggled for a minute, with Caleb taking a few blows to the face, while she twisted her body and pulled his shoulder to the right. He lost his balance and fell to the floor.

"Damn, Caleb. That was too easy," Simon mocked. "I would have jumped in to help you, but she took you down too quickly."

"I'm still not going to hit her," Caleb said, "but great job, Leah." He looked around at the coven. "We need to be able to fight with our hands and not rely on magic. The amount of training we've done this year has helped us more than simply practicing our magic all these years. Our physical strength will sometimes be our saving grace. But we need more training."

"*You* need more training," Leah mocked and giggled to herself.

My phone rang and I turned from the group. "Hey, Joel. I was going to call you after we finish training," I admitted before he started speaking.

"Lily told me what happened to Tippy. What did you guys find out?"

I explained to Joel what Melissa had discovered about Tippy's body and the recent updates on The Black Horse clan, but I was only met with silence on the other end of the line.

"Joel?"

"Sorry. I'm just thinking," he said. I heard Derek in the background saying something, but I couldn't make out what it was. "I'll do some digging around on my end, but don't do anything until I find out more. Okay?"

"Sure. Got it," I lied, knowing we were going to that club tonight.

After hanging up the phone, I turned to Caleb. "I need Sarah if I'm going to go to that club." I took my gloves off and tossed them back into the bag. "You guys keep practicing. I'll send her a text now."

Caleb turned to the rest of the coven, and they paired up again. Ezra was happy to be the one attacking Leah this time, as he had no problem throwing a punch at her. I respected that. We weren't fragile girls. We were vampire hunters.

I typed out a text to Sarah to let her know about our plans tonight.

Me: *Hey, can you make me a blonde tonight?*

I waited a minute before she responded.

Sarah: *Oh, boy, what's going on?*

How do I put this without freaking her out?

Me: *There's a new vampire club in Providence. I need to scope them out. We think it might be tied to the murder in East Greenwich.*

Sarah: *Yikes, okay. I'll be there at eight.*

Well, that was easy. Last time we went to a vampire lair undercover, someone had almost kidnapped her again. I hated putting her life in danger, but she was adamant on helping us because she had a power none of us possessed.

I dried off the remaining water from my legs, then I heard a knock at my bedroom door.

"Come in. I'm in the bathroom," I shouted.

I didn't need to mess with makeup or do my hair, as we had that one covered. After my Awakening, Joel had performed a spell on me to mask my scent, as it was luring vampires to me left and right. It worked out perfectly to go undercover in the vampire underworld so we could take out the ones that were killing the innocent or had planned to. It also helped me find the vampires who yearned to be human again so I could change them back.

After a few months, the plan wasn't working anymore. They knew of my existence, and they knew my face. Every time I'd get close, they'd run like scared little rabbits.

Sarah always had a plan, and this one was brilliant.

"Okay, what look are we going for tonight? You said blonde, right?" she asked.

I nodded. "Blonde, short pixie cut. Give me blue eyes and bring them in slightly. Make them rounder, too . . . oh, and bigger boobs."

She and I busted out laughing. "This really is my favorite part of the weekend," she said.

Sarah placed her hands on my face and chanted for a minute, and when she removed them, she clapped to herself. "Look at you!" She turned me around to face the bathroom mirror. She really did wonders with her power. Although I could control all the elements, I didn't have every power there was, but thankfully, we had a nice balance of what we could do between our coven and our fellow witch allies.

"Now, just like before, you can't be more than twenty feet from me, or the spell wears off." She pulled out a sexy, red spaghetti-strap dress from her bag. "Wear this."

The dress was stunning. I didn't dress up much, but the occasional night out when I could put on a little more makeup than usual and wear a cute dress was fun.

"What are you wearing?" I asked as she pulled out another dress, this one teal blue and strapless with sequins lining the bottom. "Pretty. It matches your eyes."

"Thanks," she said. "Now, off to get cute." She bundled up the dress and padded to the bathroom, shutting the door behind her.

Footsteps rounded the corner outside the bedroom walls. I turned around as Caleb entered.

"Mercy?" he asked as our eyes met. Sarah always made me look different each time she cast a spell on me, so this face was new and unfamiliar to him.

"Yeah, it's me."

He sized me up and placed his hand on the top of my head, following the blonde strands down to my chin with his fingertips. "Be careful tonight," he warned. "From what I've heard, this clan is ruthless." He let go of my hair and looked over toward the bed where the red dress was spread out. "Are you wearing *that*?" he asked, his tone harsh and judgmental.

"Yes, Caleb. I'm wearing *that*." I rolled my eyes and moved toward the dress. I held it up and smiled to myself. "It's beautiful, isn't it?"

"You're supposed to be inconspicuous, remember?"

"Yes, I know, but I also need vampires to open up to me, so I need to look hot." I placed the dress on the bed again.

When I turned back around, he had stepped an inch closer and placed his hand on my cheek, caressing my soft skin under the pad of his fingertips. I stiffened and backed up. "Stop, Caleb," I warned, but he only moved closer, closing the space between us.

"Still nothing, huh? Just like that." He snapped his fingers and frowned

"Are you back to this again?"

He stared at me, but it was distant. He lowered his brows and closed his eyes. "It was so *selfish* of you," he said before opening them again. His hurtful words caused my body to tense.

I balled my hands into fists as a rush of heat coursed through my body. Just hearing those accusatory words come out of his mouth made my heart pound hard against my chest, and for a moment, I felt my powers tremble inside of me, just begging to come out. "It was the most selfless thing I've ever done. I remember feeling something for you," I admitted, still not relaxing my fists. "I *still* remember it. All the memories and all the love we once shared. The memory of it all is still there."

I finally relaxed when those words left me, as if I had been holding in a deep breath. It calmed me, but only enough for my heartrate to slow down and for my hands to relax. I was still angry that he was bringing this up again, especially now. Did I have to hurt him so badly that he'd finally let it go and leave me alone?

"I sacrificed my feelings for you and Dorian for the greater good of the coven and everyone who relied on us to protect them," I said, while trying not to glare so intently into his eyes. Those beautiful eyes that were the most intoxicating sight I had' ever seen. Sometimes it was hard to look away, but I had to. I looked down. "I don't regret it. I don't regret any of it." A stabbing pain ached in my chest as those words left my mouth.

"Mercy—"

I held up my hand. "I also remember the lies. I remember the deception you showed me over and over again for your own selfish needs. Even if I could reverse this spell and fall in love with you all over again, I wouldn't. I don't *want* to love you!"

I knew my words cut through him like a knife. Those words may have been the worst thing I could have ever said to him. But I didn't know any other way to get through to him. It had been a year. He needed to move on.

"We are a coven, Caleb, and that is all we will ever be to each other."

I didn't mean for the words to come off so harshly. Of course he was more than just a coven member to me. He was a friend and even as close as family, but it had been a year, and he still hadn't stopped fighting for us to have what we had so long ago.

His face was unreadable, his mouth set in a flat line. He turned away from me as we heard the bathroom door open.

Sarah appeared from the bathroom, with her brown hair curled in tight waves and her dress snug against her thin frame, with high, silver heels. "What did I just walk in on?" she asked.

I shook my head. "Caleb was just leaving."

He glanced at me, but only briefly. His eyes stayed on her as if I were no longer in the room. "If you two don't text me on the hour, every hour, I'm coming out there to get you."

I had hurt him so badly that he couldn't even respond to what I had just said. He wouldn't even look at me.

Caleb stormed out, slamming the door behind him, which caused me to jump back. "I really hurt him this time."

"Can you blame him? He's been in love with you for over

three hundred and twenty years."

After Tatyana had rescued Dorian, all hell had broken loose at the lair where Maurice had held me captive. Maurice and Kyoko fled and went into hiding, but rumors had spread across the supernatural world that he and Kyoko had taken off to the west coast. All the vampires that lived there had left to find a new clan, and the humans had finally been set free.

Dorian and Noah stayed together, and it took me several days to track them down. Once I found them, I'd looked him in his eyes, just as I had with Caleb, and I'd told him what I had done, and what I felt. He understood why I had done it, but I still hurt him. The only communication I now had with Dorian were a few text messages every month to check in with each other and to let the other know we were safe.

That was our agreement.

I had offered Dorian my wrist to drink from that night, but he'd refused. He'd said he wanted to stay a vampire, so that if I ever needed saving, he could be there for me to fight by my side.

I eyed the clock. "We have to go. The club opened an hour ago. Roland had his friend Marcus put our names on the list, so we shouldn't have a problem getting underground."

"Let's go, then," Sarah said, grabbing my hand. "If anything goes south, I'll turn you back so you can fight in your own skin."

I smiled at her. "Damn straight, I will."

CHAPTER FIVE

"**I**Ds," a burly man at the entrance of The Black Horse said.

We handed him our drivers' licenses and as he looked down at them, Sarah used her powers to manipulate the way the bouncer saw my photo, and she changed my birthday while he scanned them over. I always carried my fake ID around, but we didn't have time to make one for this new face.

He looked at us and back down at our pictures. When he didn't let us in right away, I got an empty feeling in the pit of my stomach. What was he looking for?

Just let us in.

"Hold out your wrists," he finally said.

A smile reached my face as all the tension I had been holding in was released. He wrapped a black wristband around each of our wrists, stepped to the side, and gestured for us to go in.

The music was so deafening, I had to lean in close to Sarah's ear in order to talk to her. "We need to find a guy named Marcus," I told her.

"What does he look like?" she shouted.

"Middle-aged black man, grey suit and red tie. He's Roland's buddy!" I shouted back in her ear.

"Vampire?" she asked.

"Witch, actually." I looked around the room. "Roland said we could trust him." I raised one eyebrow.

"Ah, you don't, do you?"

"No. I'm not sure. I still don't trust Roland completely, but it's not like I can flat out tell Caleb that."

"Let's keep an eye out and tread lightly," Sarah said.

We scanned the bar but didn't see him. "Let's get a drink," I shouted over the music.

The two of us didn't drink, but not having a drink in our hand would look suspicious inside a bar, especially since we weren't even dancing, so we each ordered a cocktail and pretended to sip it.

Over in the corner of the bar, leaning up against green velvet curtains on the stage, was a cute blond-haired guy, staring at us.

"Three o'clock," I said.

She turned toward the stage. "He's hot. Looks human." She turned back to me and shrugged, "Though, I've been wrong before. Talk to him. See what you can find out," she said with a grin. She nudged me, and I skipped in his direction, just as the music changed to a song I didn't recognize, and thankfully, it wasn't as loud.

I looked over my shoulder as Sarah sauntered closer so we could stay at least twenty feet from each other. She sat down in a booth near the stage and pretended to drink her cocktail.

"Hi. I'm Cassy." I held out my hand for him to shake.

"I'm Devon. Nice to meet you, Cassy." He shook my hand and looked down at my drink, "What are you drinking?"

"Cranberry and vodka."

"Does it not taste good?" he asked.

"What do you mean?" I asked with an uncertain tone.

"I've seen you *pretend* to drink it, but not actually drink."

Observant.

I didn't hate the taste of alcohol, but we found that drinking too much weakened our abilities, so we avoided it if we were in situations where we'd need to use our powers, even a sip. If I didn't drink now, and this guy was in cahoots with the vampire clan beneath us, he'd know something was up.

I sipped my drink and flashed him a fake smile. "I was just taking it slow. I'm a light weight."

Devon smirked at me, then turned toward a pretty brunette walking by us. I had used this opportunity to mouth the word, "drink," to Sarah, but my eyes narrowed in on her empty glass. There was no way she drank it that fast.

"Yeah." His voice pulled my attention back to him. "Most girls can't handle what we men can put down," he said.

This guy is something else.

He grabbed my glass. "Another?" he asked. I looked down at my drink and it was empty. I looked over at Sarah, and she smiled with a shrug.

Ah, she's making it appear empty. I'm sure if I stuck my finger in the "empty" glass, I'd feel the cocktail.

Devon set my full glass on the counter, which he saw as empty and walked toward the bar. A minute later, he came back with another cocktail and a beer for himself.

We clinked our glasses and both sipped our drinks.

"How about we go downstairs and talk," he suggested.

"The underground club?"

"Ah, you know about the club?"

"We're on the list," I said, tossing in a wink.

Devon smirked and grabbed my hand. "Let's go."

After Sarah introduced herself as Mandy, he gestured to a hallway that led to the back of the bar. "After you, ladies."

The hallway that led to the club wrapped around but also descended underground. We came to a door with a shade on it that lifted when Devon knocked three times. A pale-faced woman appeared in the little window.

"State your name," she said.

"Devon Nordac." She waited. Devon placed two fingers on his neck and turned to me. "They're with me," he told her.

"State your names," she repeated.

"I said they're with me," he shot back, his tone harsh and elevated.

"Cassy Thomas and Mandy Rain," I told the woman at the door, and both of us placed two fingers on our necks. She looked down at a sheet of paper and back at us. She closed the window flap, and we waited.

Devon turned to us and shrugged. The door opened, and the tiny woman appeared in the doorway, gesturing for us to enter. Once inside, we looked around. Colored lights were flashing all around us, but the music was thankfully not as loud as it was upstairs.

I took another sip of my cocktail, but just enough to show Devon I was, indeed, drinking. I leaned toward Sarah's ear. "Let's dance for a few minutes before we snoop."

"I like the way you think, Mercy ... I mean, Cassy." We both laughed, and I looked around to see where Devon had gone, as he was no longer standing by us. "Where did he go?" she asked.

I turned toward another stage where the DJ was stationed and spotted Devon talking to a man in his mid-forties, who was good looking and appeared to be tall. He was sitting on a red leather chair at the end of the club, legs outstretched, and beautiful, pale women surrounded him. "Over there." I nodded their way. "Let's move closer."

We didn't need to be sneaky, though. Devon caught our attention and waved us over.

This is too easy.

I didn't get less than ten feet near them before the middle-aged man he had been talking to locked eyes with me and visions came rolling in.

Here I go.

The man was running by my side in a field next to my old home in Salem. I looked about six years old.

"Try to grab one, Mercy. Over here."

I looked above me as fireflies swarmed around us. I lifted a copper cup and a few fireflies landed inside, so I cupped the top with my hand to keep them from flying away. "They're so pretty, Papa," I said, and my vision came back to the beat of Ellie Goulding's song, *Lights*.

"Cassy!" I heard Devon shout, and I realized I was still gawking at this man I now knew as my father from the seventeenth century: Alexander.

"This is Alex. He owns the club," Devon explained.

I looked over at Sarah with my jaw clenched. I had to turn away from them because I was having a hard time concealing the shocked look on my face.

Sarah held up a finger. "Sorry, guys. Please give us a minute." She gripped my arm and pushed me over to the side.

"What the hell was that?" she asked.

"We need to go, Sarah. Now!"

"Wait, why? Who is it?"

"It's my father."

"Deadbeat dad?"

"No, that man sitting on that chair is my father from my past life. Alexander," I explained, running my hand through my hair. "He looks a bit different than he did back then. I've had visions of him before, but they were brief. Vampires kidnapped him when I was sixteen." I looked over at him and he was staring at us, along with Devon.

Dammit. We need to leave.

Sarah shook her head. "It's not like he'll recognize you.

We came here to find out more about this clan, and what better way to do it than getting in close with their leader?"

"My father!" I corrected, practically shouting.

"Shhh! Jesus, Mercy. Get it together."

"Okay. Okay." I looked over and smiled. "We've already drawn enough attention to ourselves since we've been here, so let's make the connection and leave."

She nodded and grabbed my hand, leading me back over to Devon and my father.

"Welcome back," Devon said.

Alexander stood and reached out his hand. I held mine out and he delicately grabbed it and kissed the top. I gulped and felt a hard lump slowly move down my throat. Sarah gave him her hand, and he did the same with her.

"Welcome to my club, ladies," my father said. "Drinks are on the house. Devon is my right hand, so anything you need, just ask him."

If I wasn't so overwhelmed with nerves, I would have been excited about the fact that we happened to make "friends" with the leader's right hand.

Devon then gestured to the bar, and we followed. "Here's some water." He handed Sarah and me each a bottled water. "It gets a lot hotter down here than the rest of the club, so you need to hydrate. Those cocktails won't do it."

We thanked him and drank at least half of our waters before we worked our way to the dance floor.

As we met at the center of the club, I spotted Roland's

friend Marcus standing against the wall by the bar. "Wait here," I told her.

Marcus wasn't far from where we were standing, so the distance kept me close enough to Sarah so her spell didn't wear off.

"Marcus?" I asked him. He nodded and gestured for me to follow him, but I shook my head. "Right here is fine." I glanced over at my father and Devon to make sure they weren't watching us, which they weren't.

Turning my head back to Marcus, I felt a wave of vertigo. I blinked and tried to focus so I could pull my attention back to him. It *was* hot in here, and the heat was obviously getting to me.

"Roland said you're the guy I should talk to." I quickly glanced at Sarah, who was now dancing with Devon. He placed his hands on her hips as she moved back, grinding into him.

What the hell is she doing?

"I am," Marcus answered, pulling my attention back to him.

"Sorry, Marcus. I need you to make up a story about how we are best pals and make us permanent members of this club. Keep us on the list and tell them we're humans with connections." I paused, a smile forming on my lips. "Oh, and tell them that I love to let vampires drink from me."

"That's a great way to get caught," he pointed out. "Once they start noticing their vampire clan is getting smaller, your plan is over."

I laughed. "You underestimate me, Marcus." I winked at him and took a step back. "Gotta go rescue my friend. We'll be in touch."

As I walked toward Sarah, my head pounded, and a wave of nausea hit me. Dizziness took over.

When I reached her, her hair was sticky with sweat, and mascara was smudged around her eyes. She looked dazed.

"Hey, are you okay?" I asked her. When she didn't respond, I said, "I'll go grab us some more water."

"How about some fresh air instead?" Devon suggested, grabbing Sarah by the arm and gripping mine firmly, just as I was about to collapse to the floor. He helped keep us both steady and walked us toward the back of the club. His grip on my arm tightened.

I felt my dress loosen around the chest and when I looked down, my breast size was shrinking, "Oh, no," I mumbled to myself.

As we walked past a mirror on the hallway wall, I quickly glanced up. Sarah was losing control of the spell. My hair was getting darker as we walked by the window, but thankfully, Devon hadn't looked down at me yet. We stumbled through a doorway, and I looked over at Sarah, whose eyes were shutting. She was clearly not herself, either, as she lost her balance and almost fell over. I barely caught her before she hit the ground, but almost stumbled myself as Devon still had a firm grip on my arm.

Oh, great. The asshole drugged us.

"Right here, ladies." Devon gestured toward a black,

leather sofa. When I looked up, he grinned at me, flashing his perfectly white teeth. This creep was a rapist, and he was not going to get away with this.

Not tonight.

Not to anyone, ever!

A moment later, I heard the unbuckling of his belt. I couldn't hold Sarah's slouching body anymore, so I slowly lowered her to the couch next to us.

The curtain at the back of the room shielded us from the rest of the club.

Great.

I looked around and back up at him. My head was fogging over, and nausea reached the top of my throat.

"Look at you, Cassy. If that's even your real name. I *am* digging the long, dark hair much better than the blonde," he said, trailing my long strands with his fingertips, creating a bitter tang in my mouth, and a rush of nausea hit my throat again.

"Go to hell," I said, but my threat came out weak and shaky.

He laughed and grabbed my knee. "It's a shame your chest is getting smaller. They looked great on you."

I jerked my leg away and looked at Sarah. "Sarah, wake up," I cried while ignoring his rough hand, which landed on my knee again. "Look, scumbag," I managed to mumble out through a shaky breath. "I don't think you realize what you've gotten yourself into. If I were you, I'd think twice before you touch us," I warned. The room was spinning, and all I wanted to do was close my eyes. But if I did, he would violate us both.

Devon was on me before I could throw out another threat. He pushed me hard against the back of the couch, straddled both sides of my thighs, and squeezed his legs together, pinching my hips with his knees so I couldn't move. I put my hands up to blast him away with my powers, but nothing happened.

No! I need to fight harder.

Panic rose in my chest, and my stomach felt like a hard rock was pressing up against it. I wanted to curse him out again, but I couldn't form the words. I had never been this scared, and I most certainly had never felt this helpless.

We will not be raped.

"Are you a human?" I asked, while he placed his hands on my chest and proceeded to touch my body, gliding his hands up and down my breasts.

He didn't answer me. He simply opened his mouth and fangs protruded. "Seeing as how you disguised your appearance, my only guess is that you're a witch." He glanced over at Sarah. "Or she is."

Just drink from me, rapist.

I waited for the bite to come, but it never did. "Just drink from me," I said, hoping me asking him would entice him, but he was only interested in one thing, and it wasn't my blood. His hands were now by my thighs, pulling up my dress.

I froze.

No!

I screamed in my head over and over again. Anything but this.

My body was completely paralyzed. I closed my eyes and tried to go to another place, but suddenly, his hands left my thighs and the pressure against my hips released. When my eyes shot open, I saw Devon shoot across the room with a trail of flames behind him. I turned to the doorway and Caleb was standing there, fire blazing from his fingertips, and his eyes were brighter than I had ever seen them.

In that moment, I thanked God I had forgotten to text him on the hour that we were safe.

CHAPTER SIX

"**D**id you kill him?" I asked as I awoke in Caleb's bed the next morning.

When he didn't respond, I looked at him and an unsettling feeling hit the pit of my stomach.

Caleb's hands rested on his face, his elbows on his knees. His shoulders slumped, and when he finally looked at me, his stare was empty and distant. The last time I had seen Caleb like this was when I told him we couldn't be together.

He wouldn't answer, so I pressed for another question. "Where is Sarah?" I just needed to hear him speak.

"She slept in the guest bedroom downstairs," he said finally.

She was safe. We were both safe.

"Is she okay?" I asked.

He nodded. "I think so. She hadn't woken since I had laid her into bed, so you'll want to talk to her when she's awake. I slept in Roland's room. He's still out of town," he explained as if he had been reading my thoughts. He probably assumed I thought we shared a bed together. I wouldn't have cared; we had just slept. I trusted him with my life.

"Does the coven know where I am? They'll worry since I didn't come home."

He nodded and moved in my direction. He laid down next to me, but created enough distance so we didn't touch. "Yes, he's dead. After his body turned to ashes, I swept him outside the back door into the parking lot. Your cover isn't broken. He'll just be a missing person to them."

"To my father," I corrected. I watched as his expression turned from somber to surprise as his brows raised.

He pursed his lips and blinked. "Your father?"

Still staring at him, I said, "Alexander is alive." His eyes grew wide.

He tipped his head to the side. "He was there?"

"He's their leader and the owner of the club," I explained. "He never knew it was me, though. The spell Sarah cast didn't fade until we left the main dance floor. He didn't see me transition back."

"Good," he said, letting out a heavy breath. "But this changes things a bit, doesn't it?"

"No. I'm not going to let emotions change things. He is a vampire who runs one of the most dangerous vampire clans on the east coast. I won't hesitate if I have to kill him," I said.

Caleb's phone beeped, pulling his attention away from me. I waited as he read an incoming text message, then turned to face me again.

"It's Melissa. She found a fresh tattoo on the inside of Tippy's lip. She thinks it was done postmortem by the person who killed him. She's sending me the image now."

We waited a minute and the image came through. He clicked on it, opening it to its full size. It was a black horse with red eyes. We looked at each other and back at the image. "A vampire murderer is leaving us a signature. That's a new one for us," I said.

"At least we were right about who's doing this." Caleb closed down his phone. "It's obvious that whoever did this wanted us to know he's part of The Black Horse clan. They're drawing you out," he said. "Let's be one step ahead."

"We always are."

My phone rang, but I didn't answer. I didn't even look down to see who it was. "I don't want to train today," I said. "My body feels fine, of course, but after last night, I—"

"I know. I mean, I don't know what you're feeling, but I understand. No training today." He shifted his body to face me, nuzzling his neck into the pillow. "I wanted to kill everyone in that club last night after I saw what he was going to do." He closed his eyes tightly, and when he opened them back up, the amber in his eyes was brighter, more vibrant. "You mean more to me than anyone or anything in this world."

"I know." I placed my hand on his cheek, but as soon as I touched his skin, he shifted to turn away from me and sat up on the bed. He was upset . . . again. "I care about you, Caleb," I said. "Taking my feelings away didn't take away my humanity. I am still a human being who feels things."

He scooted off the bed and looked down at me, but I stayed down with my head still on his pillow. "I have somewhere I have to be," he said. "Stay as long as you need. I drove you back in my car last night, but I had Sarah's car towed here."

"I'll leave her the keys and order a driver to take me home," I explained.

He nodded, but wouldn't look at me again. My heart ached as he walked away. It killed me to see him in this much pain. As I heard the front door shut, my mind immediately drifted to the day I left him alone in front of my house. Everyone had been waiting for me inside.

After I took away my feelings for him, Caleb had fallen to his knees, his knees digging into the driveway gravel, but he didn't move. I didn't feel the need to comfort him or tell him it was going to be okay. For him, it was never going to be okay. Nothing I said would have mattered.

My phone rang again, pulling me out of my memory, and this time, I looked down. It was Dorian.

Dorian!

Why was he calling? We'd agreed he'd never call me; only text messages.

"Hello?" I said, my voice shaky.

"Mercy, it's Noah."

My heartrate sped up, and butterflies fluttered my stomach.

"Noah, what's going on? Why are you calling from Dorian's phone?" I asked, panicked.

"Dorian's fine. He needs you, though. Can you get to Three Brother's Tavern after sundown?"

"Of course I'll meet him."

Noah snickered on the other line.

"What?" I asked.

"He's just really excited to see you."

I rolled my eyes. "Bye, Noah. Tell him I'll be there at six."

I hung up and headed for the shower. After getting ready, I sent a text to Laurie to let her know I'd swing by tomorrow afternoon to help with a few household items and take Cami out.

As I exited the mansion, I glanced at Sarah, who slept peacefully in the downstairs bedroom. She was stronger than most, but I knew after last night, she'd need some time to process what had happened and had almost happened.

I sent her a text to call me when she awoke.

When I entered Lily's Café, I spotted Bradley sitting at a table toward the back with a book in his hand.

"Hey, what's going on?" I asked.

He placed the book down on the table and looked up at Lily, who had just finished helping a customer. "After she locks up the shop, we'll head to Salem Harbor."

I looked through him as the realization registered with me. We had spread my mother's ashes over Salem Harbor. I looked down at my phone and eyed the date on my clock.

His eyes widened, and he placed his hands in his lap. "I'm so sorry. I thought that was why you were here."

I shook my head. "I understand why she didn't tell me. It's fine."

Lily interrupted us. "Hey, Mercy. What brings you here? We were just heading to go do some shopping."

"I'm coming with you to Salem Harbor," I said, cutting her off from continuing her lie.

Her eyes went wide, and she glared at Bradley. He looked down as if she scared him. It's not his fault she was keeping this from me.

I killed my mom a year ago today. I missed her, regardless of what she did to me. Being there where we laid her ashes would be hard, and I did understand why Lily didn't want me to go, but I hated that I wasn't given a choice.

"I'm sorry. I didn't know if you wanted to go."

I stood and walked to the cash register, and Lily followed. When I turned around to face her, I asked, "Do you blame me for her death, Lily?"

She gasped. "No. God, no. Mercy, you did what you had to do, but I know you blame yourself for what happened. You could barely stand the last time we were there when we put her ashes in the harbor. I didn't think you could handle it, especially with everything going on right now with you and the coven."

I secured my purse over my shoulder and flashed her a warm smile. "I want to go."

When she smiled back, Bradley, who had been watching us from across the café, walked toward us and handed Lily her keys.

As hard as this was going to be, I had my family to get me through it.

***

We picked up Joel on the way, who looked surprised to see me in the car, but I flashed him a smile, hoping it would help everyone relax and stop being so weird around me.

Once we reached Salem Harbor, we hurried over to the lighthouse where we sprinkled her ashes and sat on the rocks.

For the next hour, we talked about her life before she started changing into someone we didn't recognize. Because Bradley was with us, we had to tread lightly when we spoke about my mom. For all he knew, she had a mental illness and died of a brain tumor. We actually weren't far off from the truth.

"I wish I had known her," Bradley added.

"You would have liked her. She was a huge fan of Star Trek," I said, giggling under my breath.

"I like Star Wars," he said, and everyone busted out laughing, except Bradley. I laughed so hard that tears welled up in my eyes. I wasn't sure if the tears were from grief or happiness, but either way, the sudden change in my mood was what I needed to relax and not care about anything else.

"You're such a nerd, sweetie, but I love you," Lily said, squeezing his hand. He finally joined in on the laughter, but I could tell there was a slight discomfort beneath it all.

"Well, they *are* different," Bradley said, and this only made us laugh harder.

I tapered off my laugh and stood up, wiped the tears from my eyes, and walked toward the water. I placed my hand on top, my fingers lingering above the water, and swished around. "Goodbye, Mom. We'll be back in a year."

Joel and Lily suggested we grab a drink or two before heading back. Bradley didn't drink much, so he volunteered to drive us home. I handed the bartender my fake ID, and she made my cocktail. I knew I should keep my drinks to a minimum today, but I didn't expect to face any vampires right now, and I really needed that drink.

"We should have teleported," I suggested, once I had downed my third cocktail.

"True," Joel agreed. He and Lily snickered. They were about four beers in and obviously drunk.

"We should probably get going, guys. We're going to hit traffic," Bradley said.

We all agreed, closed out our tab, and headed toward the parking lot.

As we neared the car, it dawned on me that I had to meet Dorian in less than two hours. "Hey, Bradley. Can you drop me off at Three Brother's Tavern? I'll get a driver home after that."

Lily looked at me.

I smiled, wondering how she'd take this. "Dorian wants to meet with me."

She smirked. "Really?"

I shot her my best fake smile. "It's nothing. He just wants to talk."

"Uh, huh," Lily mumbled, narrowing her eyes at me.

I rolled my eyes. "Stop. Goodness, he hasn't seen me in a year, and here I show up buzzed as hell."

"Oh, you're drunk," Lily teased.

"I have two hours to sober up. Let's go."

As I climbed into the car, my eyes darted to a restaurant on the other side of the street. I was tipsy at this point, maybe even drunk, but I could have sworn I saw Maurice.

Maurice!

My stomach lurched, and I tapped Lily on the shoulder. "Lily, it's Maurice," I said as I pointed to a man sitting at a table with another woman inside the restaurant. I shook my head, squinting my eyes again. Was I just being paranoid?

"There's no way he's still in Salem," Lily said, pulling my attention toward her. "You all agreed that his threat was empty and he'd be long gone by now."

I looked in that direction again, but the man I thought was Maurice was gone. The sun shined brightly outside, so, rationally, I knew it wasn't him. He'd have burned up.

I had to be seeing things, so I shook off the thought and got in the car.

CHAPTER SEVEN

I entered the Tavern and spotted Dorian sitting in the corner booth. I had gone from wasted to extremely buzzed and I didn't want him to see me this way, so I focused on walking straight and prayed he wouldn't notice.

His head was down and his fingers lightly tapped the table. As I approached, I noticed he looked a bit different from the last time we had seen each other, a year ago. His hair was slightly longer, almost to the bottom of his ears. He wasn't wearing all black like he always did. Today, he wore a red t-shirt and blue jeans, and he sported light scruff above and below his mouth. He almost looked normal. I would never pin him as a vampire, but maybe that was his point.

As I sat down and barely missed the seat, I caught myself and scooted down the booth. He chuckled. "Have you been drinking?"

I huffed. "No." I fidgeted with my fingers under the table. "I had a few drinks a couple hours ago, but I'm fine." He opened his mouth to speak again, but I cut him off. "Is everything okay? Why did you have Noah call?"

"You asked me not to." He smiled, his lips pinched together as if trying to hold back a laugh.

I kicked him hard under the table, and he winced.

"Dorian, that's not funny. I thought something bad happened to you."

"Did you worry about me?" he asked. "Can you even feel concern for others?" I didn't think he meant for those words to come off so harshly, but it hurt to hear them, especially coming from Dorian. He did seem to be genuinely curious about the spell when I'd first performed it, and I didn't give him that much of an explanation when I told him what I had done.

"Just because my romantic feelings are gone doesn't mean I don't care about you. I'll always care about you, Dorian."

That was deep. Too deep for us right now. It had to be the cocktails talking because, though I truly cared about Dorian and Caleb, I avoided telling them. I didn't want them to get the wrong impression and think there was any way to win me back. Especially since I wasn't able to give either of them my whole heart.

A slight smile pulled at his lips. And that was exactly why I should not have said that. He was pleased with what I said, though I hoped he understood there was no hope for us.

"Why am I here, Dorian? And where have you and Noah been living?"

He ignored my questions and waved down a waitress. Once she came to our table, she handed Dorian a menu. "She'll be ordering," he told her, handing the menu over to me.

I looked up at her. "Just a coffee, please." I handed her back the menu.

She huffed. "Are you sure? We've got a lot to choose from. We've got burgers, and breakfast is all day. We even have salads—"

"Just coffee," I said.

She squinted, snatched the menu from my hands, and walked off toward the kitchen.

"I heard about what happened in East Greenwich," Dorian said.

I studied him for a few seconds before I asked, "How did you know about that?"

"Sarah called me. She felt you and your coven would need all the help you could get. Don't get mad at her."

"I'm not mad," I said. "I just didn't realize the two of you talked."

"We don't, really. Not like you think. She checks in every now and then. We did know each other the entire time she was at the lair, Mercy. She was my friend, too."

It never crossed my mind that, though she was a prisoner, she had made friends while inside, even with those deemed enemies.

I wondered how much she actually told him. I hoped she hadn't mentioned what happened last night. I still hadn't spoken to her since she awoke. She'd only sent a quick text telling me she was okay.

"You think it's that clan in Providence?" he asked, changing the subject. He probably sensed how uncomfortable this conversation was making me. Also, how much did she tell him about what was going on?

I nodded. "We think so. They just opened their club. There was also a tattoo of a black horse on the inside of Tippy's lip. That's their logo. From what we've learned, they moved here a year ago from New Orleans. They've been quiet since they came here, but the murder happened just a few weeks after the club opened. We all know when vampires are up to no good, they create a secured lair." Since I wasn't sure how much she had told him, this could be a surprise. "The leader is—" I shifted in my seat.

"Is?" he repeated.

"Alexander," I confessed.

Dorian's eyes went wide. "Didn't see that one coming."

"Yeah, none of us did."

"Let me help you. For all they know, I'm on the vampires' side. I can help get information."

I shook my head. There was no way. He had already sacrificed himself by helping me get out of Maurice's lair a year ago and almost got himself killed. I wasn't going to have his life on my hands again.

"No," I said. "It's too dangerous. We already had an incident last night, so we need to regroup and decide what we're going to do next."

"What incident?" he asked, the pitch of his voice rising a notch.

I shouldn't have said that. I didn't need him worrying about me, too.

"Nothing," I snapped. "We have it handled. Sarah shouldn't have called you."

"Let Noah help," he suggested. "He's a shapeshifter. He would be extremely beneficial to your coven."

That was one refreshing thing about Dorian. He didn't argue with me. Didn't question me when I made a decision about something. He respected it. He was also right about having Noah help us. Having as many supernatural beings on our side as possible would give us the upper hand. "I'll think about it," I said as I climbed out of the booth. He moved next to me so swiftly, my hair blew to the side. "Show off." I smiled.

He placed his hands under my jawline. The coldness from his fingers caused goosebumps to form on the back of my arms.

"Why do you have me text you, Mercy?" he asked. "If you feel nothing, why do you care so much if I'm okay?" He brushed my cheek with the back of his fingers, and slid his hands to the back of my neck, but I stopped him from inching closer to me by pressing my hand to his chest, creating a gap between us. His hand dropped to his side, and he flinched.

"Goodbye, Dorian."

"Wait, you're not driving, are you?"

"No, I'm going to call a driver."

He shook his head. "No. I'll drive you."

I wanted to leave and clear my head after our conversation, but he was being a gentleman, and with Dorian, I couldn't argue with that.

We drove to my place, and before I stepped out, I turned to him. "Thank you. And not just for the ride, but for everything."

He bit his bottom lip and placed his hand on mine. "Call me if you need us. I'm *not* texting you anymore, Mercy," he said. "I'm in your life whether you like it or not. Noah and I live near Goddard Park."

"You moved here?" I asked, surprised.

"We've been living here since Tatyana rescued us."

He had been living less than ten minutes from me this entire time, and I hadn't had a clue. I never saw him in town, so he must have been going out of his way to hide from me.

I nodded and exited the car, watching him drive away until he turned the corner at the end of the street. He was back in my life, and I wasn't sure what to think of it. Did I want this? Sure, I was happy to see him today, but I didn't know what that meant.

CHAPTER EIGHT

"Another body," Leah told me as I climbed out of the shower the next morning. I pulled my robe tight around my waist.

"What?"

"Another dead body in East Greenwich. This time, right in the middle of Main Street. It happened last night when you were out. We didn't find out until this morning," she explained.

I grabbed my phone from the nightstand, and there weren't any missed calls or text messages from Caleb. "Does Caleb know?"

"He's the one who told me." She looked uncomfortable, not making eye contact with me. "He left early this morning to meet with Melissa." She looked up when I crunched my face, and her shoulders slumped. "Sorry. I thought you knew until I realized you were taking a shower instead of joining him at the morgue."

"Thanks for letting me know."

Frustrated that I had been left in the dark, I grabbed my purse and drove to Lily's.

Once I reached a stop light, I grabbed my cell and found Sarah's number.

Me: *Hey, I know we didn't get to chat on the phone yesterday. I'm heading to Lily's, then the morgue to see what information we have for this new body that was found on Main. Are you doing okay?*

The light turned green, so I put my phone down, but I heard a message come in a minute later.

Once I reached another light, I looked down.

Sarah: *I'm still a bit shaken up, but I'll be fine. Please tell Caleb thank you for helping us that night. Let me know what you find out.*

I sucked in a breath that she was okay and dialed Lily, who picked up on the first ring. "Mercy, did you hear what happened? There's been another murder."

"I know. I'm almost to your house, then I'm going to the morgue. Are you even home?"

"Yes, we're here. Oh, Mercy, it was awful. Bradley and I were on our way to the post office this morning and we couldn't get onto Main Street. We jumped out and walked over to a police officer on the scene, and it was just like last time, except the body had already been taken away. They were taking pictures and trying to clear the street of pedestrians lurking around," Lily explained.

"Who was the victim?" I asked, my stomach twisting in knots, praying it wasn't someone I knew.

"Miss Darla," she answered.

I instantly felt sick to my stomach. Miss Darla was a widow whose husband had died five years ago. She mostly kept to herself and would never utter a cruel word to anyone. Whoever was doing this was a sick bastard. They appeared to be picking people at random. Miss Darla and Tippy had no connection to each other whatsoever. They maybe waved at each other in the marketplace, but that's it.

"Mercy?" she asked. "Are you still there?"

My attention snapped back to the call. "Yes. Sorry. I feel a little left in the dark this morning."

"I thought you knew, especially after I saw Caleb. He said you've had a hard couple of days."

She didn't ask about the club, so I assumed he hadn't told her what had happened the other night, for which I was grateful.

"I'll see you in one minute," I said before hanging up.

Though I was happy he hadn't told her about the other night, I was furious that he was keeping me away from this case. I understood he was upset about what happened at the club, but he should have called me this morning.

Bradley was washing the dishes while Lily was sitting at the table. I smiled at her, then at Bradley. "Man, you've got him whipped."

"I heard that," Bradley shouted toward us, with his back to me, scrubbing a plate.

I sat next to Lily and asked, "Are you doing okay? I know you knew Miss Darla."

"I'm sad, of course." Lily scooted her chair closer to me and placed her hand on mine. "I just don't understand why someone would want to kill her. It doesn't make any sense."

Bradley put the last plate down on the drying rack and joined us at the table. "You'd think a place like East Greenwich would be a safe haven for everyone who lives here," he said, pushing up his glasses closer to his eyes. "Maybe you should buy a gun, Lily." I looked at her and smirked, knowing she just needed the tips of her fingers to do some damage. It was beginning to be more difficult to keep this life away from Bradley, since he was always with her, but we knew we had to continue lying to him. The more we told our friends the truth, the more at risk it put them.

I tried Caleb one last time, but after another failed attempt to answer the phone, I headed to the morgue.

When I arrived, Caleb and Melissa still hadn't responded to the text I'd sent them both to open the door for me. I saw Caleb's car hidden near the back alley, so I assumed the cameras were already down. I placed my hand on the latch, and it clicked. I opened the back door and tiptoed as quietly as I could before reaching the autopsy suite.

Caleb sat against Melissa's desk, and they snickered about something. I stopped moving toward them when he placed his hand on hers, rubbing his thumb gently over her skin. She smiled and blushed. I steadied my breathing and scurried around the corner behind the wall. Though my feelings no longer existed, and I knew they were dating, since the rest of the coven told me everything, I hadn't *seen* the two of them like this.

I wasn't jealous, it was just different seeing him with someone who wasn't me, and it felt awkward to walk in on it. But I couldn't stand in the hall like this, or I'd get caught.

Walk in. Act cool.

I cleared my throat, and Caleb retracted his hand from hers. "Hey, sorry I'm late to the party." I glared at him, squinting my eyes. "Same killer?"

"Yep." Melissa pointed to Miss Darla's neck. "Same two marks." She parted Miss Darla's lips. "Same tattoo of a black horse."

I over-exaggerated my glare at Caleb since he didn't even tell me he was coming here when I awoke this morning. "Looks like I need to go back to the club."

"No!" Caleb snapped.

My body tensed. I understood he was scared something bad would happen to me again, but this was my call, and I wasn't going to be left in the dark because of one really bad night.

Melissa looked down, averting her eyes from us. She covered Miss Darla's face by zipping up the yellow bag and stepped back. "I need to go enter a few notes into the computer." She walked out, leaving me and Caleb ready to argue again.

"I'm going!" I was almost shouting this time.

"No, you're not."

"This is about the coven, Caleb. Someone is doing this to get to us, and you can't just take over and leave me out of it."

The stubbornness of my own voice made me cringe, but Caleb was so infuriating sometimes, he brought it out of me. And I hated it.

"Oh, yes, I will," he threatened.

I felt the energy building up inside me. I couldn't control it, I couldn't conceal it.

I slammed my hand onto the metal table next to me, and the energy that left my hands exploded through the room, causing every piece of glass to shatter around us and metal objects to rattle. The green energy leaving my fingertips blasted a second time without my control, shooting Miss Darla's table across the room and almost knocking her body off the table. I quickly backed up, holding my trembling hands against my chest to help keep my powers concealed.

"Holy shit, Mercy. What the hell was that?" Caleb gasped.

Melissa quickly ran in and looked around. "You guys need to go. Now. My boss is going to fire me!"

I looked at Caleb, who stood there with flared nostrils and cold eyes.

As I averted my eyes from him, I saw the mess in the room and instantly felt sick. This was the first time I'd lost my temper like that with someone who wasn't an enemy. It was as if I had no control over my powers. "I'm so sorry, Melissa. I'll clean this up."

"No! Get out. This is why I hesitated to help you guys in the first place." She pointed to the door. "Please leave."

I backed up as Caleb stared at me in disbelief. I didn't recognize the girl that just destroyed an office by the tips of her fingers. I breathed in steadily as I backed toward the door and ran outside to my car.

CHAPTER NINE

T hough Cami was far from normal, she was still the most stable thing in my life, and I needed a refreshing dose of normalcy right now.

When I walked through the door, I saw Cami sitting next to her mom.

"Hey, Laurie."

Laurie had a bottle of vodka in her hand, rubbing the sides with her thumb, when she looked up. "Hi, Mercy. You ladies . . . going . . . out?"

She was wasted.

"Yeah, I'm going to take her to Main Street to get some breakfast. Cami needs some fresh air. Don't you think?"

Laurie looked at Cami, who sat cross-legged on the couch, looking down at her phone. Cami looked up for a second, then back down.

"Cami, let's go," I said.

Cami gripped her cell. She stood, placed it into her pocket, and kissed her mom on the cheek. She had no emotion on her face, she just stared at me, waiting for the next command.

I stepped toward her and reached out my hand. She took it. "Are you okay?"

She nodded as I escorted her out of the house.

Her home was the most suffocating place I had ever been, even compared to the vampire lair I was held hostage in last year. Her mom stayed drunk, and the house was filthy. Before Cami was possessed by Kylan, she at least ran the household and took care of things. She put her mom to bed, helped her wake up in the morning, cleaned, and paid the bills. Now, I came there twice a week to sort through their mail, write and forge checks, and do some light cleaning to make sure the two of them could function. This was my obligation. I was the reason this happened to her. It was my responsibility now to make sure they were okay.

Lily's Café was only a few blocks from Cami's home, so we went there before I helped manage the house. It was the only way I could get Cami to go outside.

"I'll go get us some food," I said as we took a seat in the outside eating area.

Cami sat there, looking out at Main Street, watching each car pass by the café. She just . . . stared.

Lily had hired Jeff from my high school to run the café after my Awakening, since my focus was now on the coven.

Jeff saw me enter and perked up. After all the events from last year had calmed down, I visited his home and we talked about what had happened on the field when I had healed his broken femur. I told him everything. He had witnessed something that was beyond impossible, so there was no way I could keep it a secret. It took him a while to grasp what I was saying, and to accept this new reality where witches, werewolves, and vampires roamed the streets, but in the end, he swore to keep it a secret, and I swore to protect him if he ever needed it.

"Hey, Jeff," I said as I reached the register. "Just two bagels. One with cream cheese and the other with strawberry jam. Oh, and a soy latte."

"Sure thing, Mercy." His voice cracked and he averted his eyes and searched for our bagels in the glass case by the register. I didn't think he meant to sound so nervous and on edge around me, but after everything I'd told him about what I could do with my powers, he still acted anxious when I came around.

Jeff grabbed our bagels, and I waited while he brewed the shots for my latte. "Thanks, Jeff." He handed me the bagels. "How are things?" I asked, hoping to help him relax. "Anyone need their ass kicked?"

He laughed. "Not yet."

"Damn," I cursed and grabbed my latte. "Talk to you later, Jeff. Good seeing you." He reciprocated a nod and I went outside to join Cami.

When I came outside, Cami wasn't sitting at our table anymore.

Great.

My heart raced as I looked around. "Cami?!" I shouted, looking up both ends of the street.

This isn't good.

Cami was unstable. She never left the house without me, and now I had lost her. I ran down the road and poked my head into every shop that was open. "Cami?" I called as I looked into Mario's. I crossed the street to the other side and started with the shops.

I looked over by the post office, then scanned the street, and there was Cami, standing in the middle of the road with her arms outstretched.

Oh, my God.

The post office was the first building on Main Street, which was near the front entrance of the shops. The street came to a peak, then declined until it hit the post office. If someone was tearing down the road, they wouldn't see her until it was too late. I ran as fast as I could toward her.

"Cami, get out of the road!" I shouted, waving my hands in the air, but she wouldn't move or look my way.

I was getting close, but not close enough. A black pickup truck appeared at the top of the street and came speeding down in her direction. They couldn't see her. It would be impossible until it was too late. "Cami, move!" I yelled again.

I didn't have time. I wouldn't make it. I stopped running and pulled my hands out to the side, thrusting them forward while releasing my powers at the truck. The green light hit the truck like a head-on collision, causing it to fly up into the air. He missed hitting her by only a few feet. I used my other hand to thrust the car to the right and into the pole. I slowed it down right before it collided, easing up on impact. Cami stood still. She didn't even flinch.

Once the truck was no longer a threat, I ran toward her as fast as I could, and pulled her out of the road.

Cami had tears in her eyes but her face stayed emotion-less. "I just want this nightmare to end, Mercy. Please make it stop."

She was so broken. Several people were coming out to see what had happened. An older man exited the truck, and he didn't appear to have any visible injuries. He was just a little disoriented, probably wondering what the hell had just happened.

I pulled Cami into my arms, gripping her shoulders tightly. Cami was like a rag doll in my arms, as if she wasn't really there. Her mind was somewhere else. Somewhere dark and haunting. I wished I could see what was happening to her. I wished my healing powers could heal her mind, but they couldn't. I tried. Even when I failed over and over again to heal her, I tried.

What was happening?

I can't keep her in that house without someone watching her twenty-four-seven. Not now. She is way worse than she had been when we first brought her home.

What did Kylan's sick and twisted mind do to her? Caleb was possessed for only fifteen minutes, and he was an immortal witch. Even he had mentioned he felt off for several weeks. But Cami was a fragile human that had been corrupted by darkness for several days. I didn't know how to fix this.

"Cami, let's go home," I told her. I grabbed her hand and pulled her out of the street.

I have to admit her. We don't have a choice.

CHAPTER TEN

I sat on Caleb's bed, with my hands clasped together, waiting for him to come out of the shower and thinking about what happened with Cami.

Caleb and I had called Leah's family's hospital in Salem, Raven's Mental Institution, to have Cami admitted. She wasn't a supernatural being, but her mental state had been caused by one. If any place could help her, it would be Raven's.

I let Cami's mom know I would still go to her house and help take care of it, so she was fine with her daughter leaving. She may have been drunk half the time, but she was coherent enough to understand that her daughter needed help. After I told her what had happened on Main Street, she cried in my arms and begged me to get her help.

Since we were the reason this had happened to her, Leah and her family were covering the cost, and we'd be sending her there tomorrow morning.

I turned my attention toward Caleb's bathroom door as it opened. Caleb emerged, steam from the shower crept into the bedroom, and Caleb, with just a towel around his waist, moved to the dresser to pick out his pajama bottoms. Water still beaded on his perfect body and dripped down onto the carpet. I averted my eyes for a moment, then looked up again at him. I hated when these feelings of lust took over, when I needed to think of him as only part of my coven to focus on working together.

"Sorry about what happened this morning," I said, breaking myself away from this uncomfortable feeling.

He wouldn't look at me as he shuffled through his top dresser, looking for a shirt.

"I don't know what happened," I continued, though I didn't deserve an apology. The truth was, I really should have been kissing up to Melissa. My actions could have gotten her fired, and she had been helping us for a year.

He pulled a white t-shirt over his head. "I get it, Mercy. You're used to running things. But as a coven, we're also supposed to look after each other. Your dad being the leader of that clan complicates things. You can't be involved."

He was right, but I didn't care. Someone from my father's clan was killing people *because* of me. At least, that's what we thought. I refused to believe my own father was a murderer. He and Roland trained us to protect people, not harm them. Vampire or not, he knew right from wrong. They all did.

On the other hand, we believed by now that every vampire alive knew I was reborn. If that were true, why wouldn't he go looking for me? It would be a strange way to get my attention, but I couldn't rule it out completely.

I had a sinking feeling that another body would turn up again if I didn't go to Alexander in my own flesh. He was my father, maybe he would just tell me if it was him, or if he knew who was doing it. When bodies showed up in East Greenwich last year, it was always to draw me out. The vampires feared I was on a rampage to kill them, so they tried to outsmart me. They thought if they saw me coming, they could capture me and bury me alive. Once we agreed to a treaty with them, the body count slowed down. Whoever did this didn't get the memo, or there was something else at play.

"Okay, I won't be a part of this case," I lied.

Caleb grabbed his boxers and flannel pants, pulling them from under the towel, then dropped the towel once he was dressed. This time he watched me . . . watch him. A smile pulled on the side of his mouth, so I looked away.

Stop it, Mercy. He's enjoying this.

"You'll still be informed of what is going on. I just can't have you going back to that club," he explained.

"Yeah, I get it," I said too quickly.

"You're going to go there anyway, aren't you?" he asked.

Arguing with him was pointless. "We'll talk about this later," I said.

I stood and stepped to walk past him, but he moved into my path, blocking me from the door. As he looked down at me, my heart pounded against my chest. He wasn't just looking down at me, he was staring and examining every detail of my face.

"Move, Caleb," I demanded. "I don't want to use my magic on you, but I will."

He laughed out loud. "Oh, Mercy. I have the rest of the

coven backing me on this. We can use our magic to keep you here if we want."

I gulped and put my hands up. "Move," I warned again. My powers slowly moved up my arms and to my fingertips, lighting up the tips above my nails. "He's my father. He won't hurt me."

He looked down to my fingers and back to me, as if he found my reaction to be an empty threat.

It wasn't.

"No, Mercy. That's where you're wrong. He *was* your father. Not only is he *not* a part of your life in this century, but him turning into a vampire most likely changed how he feels about you."

"It didn't with Roland or Abigail."

"They never ran a murderous vampire clan," he said, raising his hand to touch me.

I moved back. "Don't," I warned. The light still lingered on my fingers. Now he was pissing me off. "Stop, Caleb!" I closed my eyes, clenching my jaw, feeling the energy build up inside as my anger escalated. "You need to step away from me, Caleb. Now."

He didn't move. He didn't listen. In fact, he stepped closer.

The feeling going through my body was like it had been in the autopsy suite. I'd always been able to control it. Always been able to turn it off if I wanted, but I couldn't anymore.

What is happening?

My frustration only built as I lifted my hands. The energy that left my fingertips flung him across the room and out of my path, energy still lingering above my fingers. Now on the floor, he looked up at me in disbelief. His mouth fell open, and he shook his head at me.

What did I just do?

I didn't speak. I didn't apologize. I just ran.

CHAPTER ELEVEN

Caleb

"Pick up, dammit," I cursed. "Why is she ignoring me?"

"She's ignoring all of us, Caleb. What happened yesterday with you two?" Leah moved to my side and sat next to me, placing her hand on my shoulder. I brushed it away and stood up. "Okay, tough guy. You don't need to be a jerk. We're just trying to help. I'm not saying it's your fault she ran away, but something *did* happen."

Yeah, it was my fault. I tried to stop her from leaving. What I'd learned about Mercy from this last year, was to never stop her from doing something she had set her mind to. She wasn't the same girl she had been a year ago. Too many people got hurt last year and she blamed herself. She told me after the dust settled last year that she would do whatever it took to keep the ones she loved safe. Her stubborn nature was both sexy and infuriating.

Simon joined us at the kitchen island and placed his plate of pasta down, turning to Leah. "Did you get Cami admitted?" Simon asked her.

She nodded. "She's all checked in. I have the best witch doctor working with her."

"Good," Ezra said, now joining us for breakfast. "Now we just have to focus on getting Mercy back. You know she went back to that club, right?"

I gripped my cell and slammed my fist on the table. I winced and outstretched my hand, feeling the muscles cramp up. I should have chased after her when she ran out of my room, but I let her go, and this morning she was gone. The coven never saw her come home last night.

"Caleb!" Leah yelped. "Calm down. We don't know that." She glared at Ezra. "We don't know that for *sure*, Ezra."

So help me, if she went into that club without backup, I'm going to drag her out by the hair. That girl makes me insane.

We needed to get down there now, but if she were going under a different face again, I couldn't risk exposing her stupid plan and getting her hurt. We needed to come up with something better than rolling in there, powers blazing.

"Is Sarah missing, too?" Leah asked. "We need to know if we are looking for Mercy's face, or another."

I shook my head. "I don't know. I'll call her when we're done here."

Simon, still chewing his food, said, "Well, we know she's not dead. We can all still feel her connected to us."

"She can't die anyway, you idiot," Ezra said.

"Stop. You're acting like toddlers. Go to your rooms," Leah scolded playfully, and the two of them laughed at her joke. I didn't think it was funny.

None of this was funny.

I have to find her.

I leaned over Bradley's shoulder, looking at his computer while he typed. "Can't you just hack into her cell phone server? I just need to access her GPS."

When Joel put that spell on her that shielded her blood from vampire senses, it also blocked him from casting any kind of location spell on her. Her complete presence was off the map to the supernatural world. It was both safe and dangerous. We knew it was dangerous to take her off the map, but we couldn't risk her being found by our enemy.

"Caleb, can I talk to you outside for a minute?" Lily asked. She'd been standing patiently in the corner of her office.

I let out a frustrated sigh and followed her out. I wasn't mad at her, just the situation. She seemed uneasy about us involving Bradley. For all he knew, this was just a regular missing person situation, and we knew once we located her, Bradley would go right back to being in the dark.

"He won't know anything," I promised. "I just need her location, and I'll leave," I explained when we stepped out onto her front porch.

She shook her head and fiddled with the bottom of her shirt. "The truth is, Caleb, I . . . *want* to tell him."

I should have seen this coming. She and Bradley had

been dating for a while now. It was only a matter of time before she wanted him to know the real her.

"Look, Lily. You're an adult. It's not up to me to give you permission. Only thing I ask is that you leave as much of it out as you can. He doesn't need to know everything. Maybe leave out the part about the Chosen Ones."

She nodded. "Of course."

When we rejoined Bradley, he looked at me with a huge grin on his face that reached his eyes. "Found her."

My heartrate picked up. "Where?"

"Okay, so her GPS was turned off, but I hacked into her phone and turned it back on. Once I did that, it showed her last location, about two hours ago." He pointed to his computer. "The pin marks the corner of Parker and Addison Lane in downtown Providence," he explained.

"Just as I thought." Bradley and Lily looked at me with confusion. "She's at the club."

"The Black Horse?" Lily asked, panic rising in her voice. "Do you think she was taken again?"

I shook my head. "No, she went on her own."

I cursed under my breath.

Lily paced the kitchen and looked up at Bradley. "Honey, can you give Caleb and me another minute?"

He smiled and walked out to the front porch. Once Bradley stepped outside and shut the door, my hands flew up. "That girl needs a GPS device injected into her arm."

Lily smiled and shook her head at me.

"I'm not kidding, Lily. Whether she's sacrificing herself to a clan of vampires or going under a different face, she didn't really think this one through. I've heard the rumors about this clan. They won't show her mercy." I huffed. "We need Joel. Can you give him a call and have him meet us at Joe's Bar and Grill? I don't know what she's up to, but we aren't repeating what happened last year."

My fury kept me from filtering my mouth. What was she thinking? I taught Mercy everything she needed to know when it came to fighting. She could knock 215-pound me across a room with one kick. She also knew her powers better than I did at her age. She learned quickly, and all in a years' time. But I couldn't shut off my feelings for her or my natural instinct to always protect her.

Bradley poked his head in, wiping the sweat from his nose and readjusting his glasses. "Everything okay? Should I call the police about Mercy?"

"No, babe. Everything is fine. I'll call you later, though. We're meeting my brother for coffee so we can talk about what to do about the Mercy situation. I'll see you tonight for dinner."

Bradley smiled and entered the kitchen to kiss Lily good-bye. He didn't look at me. Instead, he waved his hand in the air and walked out to his car.

Sarah informed us that she was not with Mercy, which meant she went there as herself. It was right before six when we met Joel and Derek at Joe's Bar and Grill. Derek was getting drinks for us while Joel tapped his hands on the table, trying to muster up his thoughts. "We know she wasn't taken, but we don't really know if she's in danger with Alexander. She might be careless, but she isn't stupid. Let's give her a little credit here. Maybe she has a plan." Joel looked up and saw the look I gave him that showed I really didn't think she had a plan, but I'll go with this theory for now. He continued. "Do you think she walked up to her father and said, 'Hi, I'm your long-lost, reincarnated daughter. Nice to see you again?'"

I finally was able to laugh, because that did sound exactly like something she would do.

I had my phone turned down but felt a vibration on my hip. "Excuse me." I stood up, reached into my pocket, and looked down at my phone.

Melissa: *There's been another body brought in. Same as last. Marks on the neck, and the tattoo. His name is Ned Parker. It's right outside my jurisdiction, but like we've done in the past, I was able to get the body transferred here. Police said he's a homeless man they've spotted a few times near Goddard Park.*

I closed my phone and walked back to the table. "I'm going to Providence to get her. Another body turned up near East Greenwich. I can't just sit here and wait for her to come back."

Lily shifted in her seat and turned to Joel. "We'll go with

you." She turned back to me while Joel stood, kissed Derek on the lips, and told him to head home without him.

We climbed into my car, leaving Lily's in the parking lot, and drove to The Black Horse.

When we arrived at the club, all the shades were closed and the door was locked. I wasn't sure if they slept here or not, but we were going to have to break in to find out. Lily placed her hand on the door lock, and we heard a click.

Once we entered, we noticed that the top floor was empty, so we assumed they were down in the club beneath us. We walked to the back and down the hall until we reached the door to the club. It was unlocked, so we walked right in. In the corner of the room, sitting on a bench, was a vampire, who, when he spotted us, immediately stood to his feet and gestured toward the back as if he were expecting us.

"We were wondering how long it would take you to get here," he said. "They're in the back."

I already had my hand out, ready to ignite a fireball, but I didn't feel threatened by him, so I lowered my hand and looked back at Lily and Joel, who both had their hands out, ready to use their powers if we needed to.

"I think we're okay," I said to them. They both lowered their hands.

We slowly entered, and Mercy was sitting next to her father. They both turned their heads toward us.

"I'm not leaving," Mercy said before we fully entered the room, seemingly annoyed to see us. "I'm safe. I'm sorry I didn't text you back. I should have."

Are you kidding me right now?

"Caleb, nice to see you after all these years," Alexander said while standing up and approaching me slowly. "I'm not going to hurt you, or her. Relax." His voice was eerily calm.

"I've just come here for Mercy."

Alexander smiled at me and looked at his daughter. "Mercy, do you want to leave?"

She shook her head. "No. Thanks for checking on me, guys, but like I said, I'm safe."

Was she really dismissing us? Just like that? She sat next to a man who hadn't seen her in centuries, and she already trusted him. For all she really knew, he could have been killing innocent humans to get to her. He ran a dangerous vampire clan, for crying out loud. I didn't doubt for a second that he would snap the neck of an innocent victim without hesitation.

No. She is not staying here.

"Mercy, let's go." My voice came off more authoritative than I had wanted. I didn't mean to upset her, but she wasn't thinking clearly.

She stood and walked up to me. "I'm not leaving."

I shook my head. "What has happened to you? You have a coven and a family who loves you." I looked over at Alexander, who wore a stupid grin on his face. "If you weren't over here playing house, you would have noticed that the body count hasn't stopped rising. We need you. A homeless man turned up dead in Goddard Park. It was the same as the others. Bite marks and a tattoo, of *your* club." I turned to Alexander again, seeing if he'd react to my accusation. He didn't.

He shook his head, walked up to me, and held out his wrist. "Feel that?"

I grabbed his wrist, placing my fingers near the vein.

Heartbeat.

I let go of his wrist, glancing at Mercy, then back at him. "Mercy?"

She placed her hand on my arm. "He isn't the one killing people. I fed him my blood a few hours ago. He doesn't want to be a vampire. He never has. For years, he ran this clan in order to keep the wicked vampires under control. He doesn't kill people, Caleb, but he hasn't always been in control of those in the clan who did. He is going to give it all up to help us."

Joel and Lily looked at each other and back at Alexander.

"I'm Mercy's uncle, and this is her Aunt Lily." Joel reached out his hand. Alexander shook it and turned back to Mercy, wrapping his fingers around her arm. My body stiffened when he touched her.

"We may be divided by the two different lives Mercy has lived, but we are *all* family," Alexander said as he turned to Mercy. "I would never hurt my daughter. I knew she was alive, but I wasn't ready to face her yet. I'm glad she came to me, and I'm also sorry about what happened at my club the other night. I would never have left anyone with Devon if I had known he would do something like that."

I huffed and looked away.

Mercy must have noticed my annoyance because she walked up to me and placed her hand on my chest, probably hoping it would help me relax. "My father is a powerful witch, Caleb. We could use his magic," Mercy said, and I relaxed. Not because of what she said, but because she still hadn't removed her hand from my chest, and her touch always helped me calm down. When my eyes met her gaze, she continued. "He's agreed to help us find out who is killing in East Greenwich." She turned and smiled at her father. "He can read minds."

Alexander's smile made me feel uneasy, but I listened. "Which is why having me help is crucial," he said. "If someone from my clan did this, I will know by reading their thoughts."

I wondered if that would work. Would they really allow a witch to get that close to them? They'd know right away he wasn't a vampire anymore. They'd kill him.

The vampire that had gestured for us to come in earlier entered the room. "I'm ready, Mercy."

He walked up to her and grabbed her wrist. She closed her eyes and his teeth reached for her skin.

"Wait!" I screamed.

"Caleb, it's okay," she said, holding up her hand.

I halted but raised my hand, ready to ignite a flame.

The vampire bit down, and Mercy winced, but relaxed as

he drank from her. He drank for about ten seconds and let go. He crunched his nose and looked like he was about to throw up. "It's okay. Try to hold it in." He blinked a few times and took a heavy breath.

"Wow." He looked at her, and a tear formed in the corner of his eye, slowly dripping down his cheek. "Seven hundred and sixty-five years. That's how long I've been undead."

"Do you feel it?" she asked him.

He nodded with a smile.

"I don't know where your soul has been, I just know that whatever my blood can do, it somehow brings it back," she explained.

"Thank you," he said as he turned to us. "I don't know how to explain this feeling. It's like a wave of water entered my body, while igniting every emotion, love, desire, and empathy that had been taken from me." He looked up to Mercy. "Good luck to you."

He walked out, but had his hands out in front of him, moving his fingers around. It was just like we had witnessed several times since Mercy's Awakening. It was a newly-turned human from vampire, shocked at the sudden change in their body, and feeling the blood rushing through their veins again. It was a surreal moment, and no matter how much I hated seeing them touch her and bite down into her flesh, it was a beautiful moment for everyone, witnessing what she could do.

Mercy smiled with pride and turned to her father. "Roland

is human, too, Father. With the two of you having your powers back, we can all be a family again and work together." She turned away from him and walked up to me. "I'm sorry for using my magic on you yesterday. I lost control...again. I'm also sorry I left without letting anyone know where I was going." She wrapped her fingers around mine and squeezed. "I haven't abandoned the coven, Caleb. But I knew you wouldn't let me come here alone. I had to be alone for him to hear me out. I am safe with him, and I plan to stay with him for a little while."

"Out of the question."

"This isn't up to you, Caleb!" she snapped.

"Why would you stay with him?"

"He's going to teach me how to control my powers. I don't know what is going on with me, but every time I get upset, I lose control. My father knows more about my powers than everyone here combined. I need his help. And I need you to be safe."

I knew she was losing control, but if anyone could help her, we could. I felt helpless. "I won't be able to focus, knowing you're here. With him being human now, shouldn't you be leaving this lair as soon as you can?"

"He doesn't live here. He has a home in Newport where we'll be crashing from now on. It's close to Abigail's mansion, and I'll gladly give you the address. We're heading there after my father gathers what personal possessions he has here at the club." She placed her hand on my arm gently. "See what you can find out about the body of the homeless man. Once I have more control of what is happening with me, I'll come back."

Joel had his arms folded and slowly walked up to Alexander. "And who will be running this place after you leave? Won't they wonder what happened to you and go on a killing spree? I've heard the stories of what your clan does to their victims."

"Don't believe everything you hear. No, this clan hasn't always been on their best behavior, but I've seen worse. I'll help you find out who from the clan is responsible for the deaths in your hometown, but I'm not going to worry about who's taking it over. I'll keep Mercy safe. I promise."

His promise meant nothing to me. I didn't trust him. I didn't like any of this, but I had no control of her. I never had, as much as I'd tried.

The hardest part about all this was that she didn't need me. I needed her, but she would never need me other than balancing our coven. She could take care of herself. Her powers were stronger than mine. Of course they were.

I walked up to Mercy and placed the tip of my fingers under her chin. She looked directly into my eyes. My heart was aching, but I had to let her go. Centuries of love and heartache came crashing down on me all at once. There was only one way this was going to go, and it wasn't with her in my arms again.

"I'm letting you go," I said.

"Thank you. Like I said, I'll be safe."

I shook my head. "No, I mean, I'm letting you *go*."

Her face went still as I slowly inched forward, and when I saw she wasn't resisting, I closed my lips to hers. The kiss was tender and short, then I released her. "You were right about taking your feelings away. I wish I could do that for myself with you. But I don't have the power to do it."

Her face was still unmoved as I walked away from her, Joel and Lily following behind me. I didn't know if anyone really knew what to say in that moment. All I knew was that, for the first time since she and I were fourteen years old, I was letting my heart move on.

CHAPTER TWELVE

Mercy

The door shut behind him as they left me standing there with my father's gaze on my back.

I touched my lips and turned to my father. He was waiting for me to say something, but I had no words.

I stood there, thinking about the only emotion I felt—relief. I didn't experience heartache or loss. Sure, there was a slight guilt that he would be hurting right now. I hated being the source of someone's pain, but what did he expect me to do? I'm not in love with him, and I hated that it hurt him as much as it did.

This was good. He could finally move on and be happy. Maybe find love with someone else.

"Are you okay?" my father asked me.

"I felt nothing when he told me that," I explained. "What does that say about me?"

"It says you're fulfilling the mission for which you were created. You don't owe Caleb anything."

I shook my head. "Why did Tatyana create me this way? Why did I ever have to do that stupid spell if all I am is an

Element? Why not just make me be this way from the start, with no feelings, no remorse or humanity," a small tear formed at the corner of my eye, "if I'm just an Element?"

He smiled. "Oh, Mercy. You're more than *just* an Element."

I looked down at my feet as a tear trickled down my cheek.

"What do you remember from your life before you died?" he asked as I wiped my cheek.

"Only a few visions. Caleb asked if I wanted all my memories back, but I told him my life before this needed to stay in the past. I didn't want to know."

He slid closer to me, touching the top of my hand and gripping his fingers around mine. "Mercy, our families were close. We always had been. Your mother Mary and I were blessed to represent centuries of witches who had the power to heal others by using the element of Spirit. We couldn't heal ourselves like you could, but as long as we used spells to pull that universal element, the element of Spirit was our strength.

"When Tatyana came to us, she told us about the vampire race that was growing and how we wouldn't be able to defeat them without taking the elements in themselves and putting them directly here on the earth. In human form. By taking those elements and putting them into a human body—not just inside a witch that could use them, but actually transform that element into a life force—the five families tied to those elements would be able to fight together and destroy what she had created.

"She told me that the element of Spirit that *our* bloodline would bring into the world would be the key element to reunite a vampire with their soul."

My eyes widened. "You knew?"

He nodded. "Roland and I were the only ones who knew what your blood would actually do. We kept it a secret to protect you, but one night, a vampire attacked you in a clearing outside the village. He turned human after biting you, but you didn't realize what was happening to him. His clan showed up right as the light from the sun shined down into the clearing. The vampires hid to protect themselves from the light, but the affected vampire never moved from where he stood. You thought your blood gave vampires the ability to walk in the light when the vampire stayed there soaking in the sun, shocked at what was happening to him. He took off before you could question him.

"It wasn't just you that believed it, but also his clan who witnessed it. I'm sure the vampire who was turned human was too afraid to face them if they knew, so he ran, and their clan told everyone what they had seen. The rumor had begun that the element of Spirit would allow a vampire to walk in the daylight without bursting into flames.

I shook my head. "I wondered how that rumor started."

"The element of Spirit was everything perfect in this world, Mercy. When you died, you took that element with you. It was as if you had drained the world of that power."

I frowned, grabbed my father's hand, and held it firmly. I had given myself up to my mob and allowed them to kill me all those years ago. It was my fault.

He must have seen the pain on my face because he gripped my hand tighter and a warm smile pulled at his lips.

"Tatyana also told us that you would fall in love in this life, Mercy. How could you not? You represented the soul. *You* have a soul, my sweet daughter. What is a soul without the power to love? You are not *just* an Element."

More tears formed in my eyes. I couldn't hold back anymore. I allowed myself to cry and to feel this pain.

"Did she see who I'd be with? Did she see Caleb and I fall in love?

He nodded.

"And Dorian? Was he part of that plan?"

He nodded again and released my hand.

"Just because she foresaw it doesn't mean it *had* to happen. You choose your own path, Mercy."

This feeling I had with my father, whom I barely remembered, was familiar and comforting. I had only small memories of him, and none of my birth father in this life. Alexander was the closest I now had to a father, and I felt safe and close to him in this moment, as if my memories of him never went away. I looked up at the clock, and it was almost five in the evening. "We should get going. We probably don't want to be here when the rest of your clan shows up after dark," I suggested. As we were about to walk out the door, I turned to him and asked. "Have you ever killed anyone?"

I wasn't sure if this was a stupid question. He promised he wasn't the one killing those in East Greenwich, but was he like Dorian, who did everything he could to keep himself from drinking from victims? It was like it was their nature to do it, and to them, it wasn't wrong.

"Yes," he admitted.

My heart sank. "Oh," was all I could say.

"Look, when your soul is taken from you, you lose a lot of your humanity. Some more than others. I met a girl and we thought we were in love," he said.

My jaw dropped. He killed someone he cared about?

"She told me that I could drink from her, so I did, but I couldn't stop for some reason. I've always been able to stop, but not with her. By the time I was able to will myself to let go, she was on the brink of death. What I didn't know was that she also was married. Her husband came home right at that moment, so I laid her down and ran out of the house but watched her slip away in his arms."

"Oh, my God, Dad. I'm so sorry."

He shook his head. "She was able to speak with him right before she passed. I hoped whatever they said to each other brought him comfort and her peace before she died."

I grabbed his hand and squeezed. "You have your soul back now. You're a different person. Live the life you should have always had before it was taken from you."

He smiled back, and those were our last words before we

left the club and drove to his place in Newport. I planned to hide out there until I was ready to face Caleb and the rest of the coven again. My father and I had a lot to catch up on, too, and I needed to get a grip on my powers. I wasn't sure what was happening to me, but it scared me, and I didn't want to lose control anymore, especially with those I cared for.

CHAPTER THIRTEEN

Caleb

Melissa crashed at the mansion last night. We didn't sleep together. We hadn't done *that* yet, but it was nice to hold her and feel her warmth against my bare chest.

We started the morning early, as she had to stop in the office to work for a few hours, and I needed to train with the coven.

When she entered the kitchen, she eyed the coffee I had brewed and poured herself a mug.

She carried a notebook and reading glasses. She put her glasses on and looked at the notes in front of her. "The homeless man, Ned, had been dead for over twenty-four hours before his body was found, which means Ned was killed before Alexander became human again. Alexander could have done it. We haven't had a body bitten by a vampire come in since."

The timing *was* too perfect, and now she was alone with him at his place. I tried to shake the thought and hoped we were wrong. But then again, he did live here in Newport. I could swing by in the morning and secretly check on them.

I placed my hand under her arm and rubbed the top of her skin ever so gently while she placed the notebook down, removed her glasses, and smiled back at me.

Melissa and I have talked off and on for the last few months, and though I knew Mercy wouldn't give her heart to me, a part of me felt like I was cheating on her. I held back with Melissa, never fully giving her everything I should have. I knew it probably frustrated her, but I didn't want to hurt her until I knew for sure there wasn't a chance with Mercy again.

Melissa was stunning. Her hair was long, like Mercy's, but had perfect curls that fell down to the center of her back and was a lighter shade of brown. She had beautiful rose and dragon tattoos that started at the tip of her shoulder and reached down to her wrist in a perfect sleeve. She also had a set of angel wings on her chest that signified her twin sister, who had passed away when they were born.

I didn't tell Melissa about what had happened three weeks ago at The Black Horse. I felt guilty about it for sure, but Mercy hadn't called me since I told her I was letting her go, not even a text. She was still staying at Alexander's place here in Newport, according to Leah, who *had* heard from her. Did the kiss freak her out?

Dammit.

"What are we doing?" Melissa's voice pulled me out of my thoughts.

"What?"

"This. What is *this* between us?"

Great, I didn't even know what this was. "I care about you. Let's start there."

She frowned and moved over to the side of the table, now standing closer to me. "I'd like to go on a real date. The only times we ever hang out are the occasional make out sessions at your house or when we're standing around a dead body." She smiled and placed her hand over mine. I reciprocated and grabbed her hand, rubbing my thumb over her skin.

"How about dinner tonight at La Masseria?" I asked.

"You don't have business with your coven?"

I pulled from our touch and ran my hands through my hair. "I'm just training with the coven this afternoon, but we'll be done early. I can pick you up at six forty-five."

She didn't have to persuade me. I wanted to take her out. I'd been wanting to ask her out for a long time but didn't want to face the coven's judgments or ruin what I thought would or could have happened with Mercy and me. I wasted my time on someone who would never love me when I had this gorgeous woman in front of me, who did care, this entire time.

I needed to move on.

While I drove to Melissa's, my phone beeped, and I glanced at it quickly while at a red light. Mercy's name appeared on the screen.

It was about damn time.

Mercy: *Someone broke into Alexander's home last night. It's not safe for me here anymore. I'm coming home.*

She always did have the worst timing.

Melissa opened the door wearing a lacy green dress. She had styled her hair in a braid that wrapped around her shoulder, and she smiled as soon as she saw me standing there with a single red rose in my hand. "Such a gentleman," she said, taking the rose from me. "Thank you."

I wore a sleek black suit and gray tie, and I'd shaved off the beard I had been growing the last three weeks as I nervously waited for Mercy to check in with me.

I cleared my thoughts and focused on the beautiful woman in front of me. I held out my hand, and she took it in hers.

After a few glasses of wine and La Masseria's delicious spaghetti marinara, Melissa excused herself to the ladies' room, and I took this opportunity to respond to Mercy.

Me: *What exactly happened last night?*

She responded almost immediately, as if she had typed it all out, waiting for me to respond first.

Mercy: *We woke up to broken glass near the balcony window. The room is three stories high, with no window or rooftop to connect to where the window sits, so either someone had thrown a* *rock through the window or we're dealing with something super-natural. You'd have to be Spiderman to scale that wall.*

Melissa was rounding the corner, so I typed up my last text to her for the night.

Me: *Stay at the mansion tonight. There's a house key under the blue vase by the front door. I'll turn off the alarm with my phone. Come in and make yourself at home. I'll be back by nine.*

I shut my phone down and glanced up at Melissa, who had rejoined me at the table.

"Everything okay?" she asked.

I let her know what was happening with Mercy, and given Melissa's kind nature, she showed her concern, but when I mentioned that Mercy would be staying with me tonight because of it, her body language changed instantly. Her shoulders slouched, and she bit her bottom lip. She didn't whine or share her thoughts, but I knew she wanted to say something.

The rest of the evening, I had given Melissa my attention, but my thoughts kept going back to the fact that I would see Mercy for the first time in three weeks. Yes, I was moving on, but since her Awakening, this was the longest we had gone without seeing each other.

Mercy's safety had always been my number one concern. I didn't know if this ruled out Alexander as the killer in East Greenwich for certain, but him turning human again was certainly a game changer unless, like Melissa had pointed out, he killed the last victim before he changed. But if that were the case, what was his motive? If it was to draw Mercy out, he had her within his grasp. Was it all to draw her back to him so he could return as a witch? It's not like she'd refuse a vampire who wanted to be a human again.

One thing was for certain. Whoever it was knew Mercy was at his house, and they were coming after her.

The lights were dim in the family room when I entered.

Mercy had helped herself to the fireplace, and sitting next to her on the table was a cup of hot cocoa. She must have just made it as I eyed the steam hovering over the mug. I could smell the cocoa as I neared her laying on the couch.

"Mercy." I gave her a gentle nudge. She opened her eyes and looked up at my wall clock.

"Hey, sorry. I was having a hard time sleeping, so I thought a warm cup of hot chocolate would help me sleep," she said, rubbing her eyes.

"It's okay." I watched her yawn and stretch her legs, still coming out of her sleep.

"Truthfully, this house is a bit large and haunting to be upstairs alone."

I smiled. "This house can be a bit creepy."

I grabbed the blanket that had slithered off the couch and pulled it over her. I sat down with her and she snuggled closer to me, laying her head down on my chest. My fingers rubbed her arm gently, trying not to push too hard on her boundaries. I tested the waters by kissing her on top of the head. She looked up with a smile.

I wasn't sure why she was letting me be this close to her. Maybe she kept her distance knowing I still loved her, but now that I had told her I was moving on, she was comfortable with me touching her.

"How was your date?" she asked. "You don't ever dress up like this."

I only smiled at her. She loved to call me out, but I wasn't ready to tell her who I had been with.

Not yet.

"Tell me what happened," I asked, ignoring her question.

She pushed herself up so she was sitting upright and sighed. "We had just gotten back from visiting a few of my father's old clan members. They respected him, so they welcomed us without any trouble. No one knows who would be doing this. There are a few members who have been kicked out in the last decade for being traitors, so the only conclusion he thought of was that they're trying to frame him. The other theory is that it might be a vampire who joined them last year whom I have a history with."

My eyebrows rose a notch. "Dorian?"

"No. He would never do this."

I huffed, realizing she was right, but I still hated the guy. "Then who?"

"Maurice."

My blood instantly boiled, and my hand clenched into a fist. If he were after her, he would torture her to make her pay for bringing down everything he created. "He joined them?" I asked.

"In February, right after the treaty. He and my father have been civil since Maurice joined The Black Horse. That was, until Maurice found out that Alexander was my father. He told him he wanted to kill me, and was going to find a way, then he took off, and they haven't seen him since. Our guess is that he's trying to frame my father so I will take him out, then use me in my broken state to torture or kill me." She shifted in her seat. "I know we don't have the dagger, but the fear it will be found is always in the back of my mind."

I looked away, trying not to make eye contact with her. I knew the truth would eventually come out, but I didn't want to ruin this moment with her.

"What is it?"

Shit.

I can't hide this. "Mercy, I have to tell you something."

I didn't think she meant to do it, but her body seemed to scoot further from me as if she were avoiding our touch, knowing I was going to say something to piss her off.

"Two weeks ago, I realized that, though Joel is a witch, he isn't as strong as us. If a mind-reading witch were to get to him, they'd be able to read his mind to find the dagger, and it could kill him."

She squeezed her eyes shut as if annoyed with my words.

"You moved it because you thought my father would use his power on Joel and go after the dagger."

She stood and paced back and forth. I didn't try to calm her down. I let her be angry because she deserved to be upset with me. I betrayed her and the rest of the coven by moving the dagger without talking about it first, and not telling them after I did.

"How many times do I have to tell you that my father isn't trying to kill me? Do you really think I'd be standing if he was? I just spent three weeks alone with him, and all he wanted to do was get to know me and what my life had been like these last nineteen years."

I now stood and hoped my words would help her relax. "It has nothing to do with your father and everything to do with Joel. We are the only ones who should know the location of the dagger. I didn't even tell Simon where I was going to put it after he helped me get it back."

"Simon helped you?"

I huffed. "Look, Mercy. I was a fool to have Joel be the one to hide it in the first place. Once I realized it was going to be too dangerous, I had Joel teleport me and Simon to the Santa Barbara Mission. It was in a secured safe inside the walls."

Her body tensed. "And that is exactly where it needs to return."

"No, Mercy. Everyone by now knows about the dagger. We need to protect it. They can't read our minds without us fighting back with our powers. They'd be fools to try."

She stopped pacing and looked back at me. It was as if the wheels were turning, but she couldn't find the words. My eyes darted to her hands which were balled into fists. "Where did you hide it? And don't lie to me. You're telling me where it is."

"Upstairs," I answered.

"Just upstairs?" Her hands flew up. "That sounds safe."

I frowned. "It's in a safe in my bedroom, under the floor boards. The code is 4575."

"You think that's safe enough?"

"We're the only ones who know the code."

She averted her eyes from me again.

I knew it wasn't the safest place, but protected spells don't last. Using a coded safe was the best thing we could do right now.

"I should get to bed," she said. "I'm meeting Lily in the morning, then I need to check on Laurie and take care of a few things in their home. I need to visit Cami, too. I haven't been there since she was admitted."

I flashed her a warm smile and told her I needed to get to bed myself, but when I turned toward the stairs, she grabbed my hand.

"Wait," she called out. "The other day at the club, when you said what you said, did you mean it?"

I nodded.

"Thank you, Caleb."

"You're welcome," I said. I paused for a moment before saying, "Happy belated birthday."

She released my hand and headed upstairs without discussing more of what had happened between us.

I crawled into my bed and tried to shut my mind off to get the first night's sleep in the last three weeks.

I can do this. I can let her go.

CHAPTER FOURTEEN

Mercy

I wrapped my hair into a messy bun and walked into the kitchen where Caleb was making breakfast.

"Coffee?" Caleb asked, pouring me a full mug, and placing it in front of me.

"Do you even have to ask?" I teased, grabbing the warm mug and placing it between my palms. "Thank you." I took a sip and looked up at him. He moved back over to the stove to finish cooking what looked like tofu scramble with mock sausage and a side of hash.

I giggled at how domestic he looked in the kitchen, and the fact that he was willing to eat a vegan breakfast with me. He wore plaid pajama bottoms which hung loosely from his hips and a white t-shirt.

He turned, placed a large portion of scramble on my plate, and turned back around to grab himself one.

After we ate in complete silence, my phone buzzed next to me. I looked down and saw a text from Dorian. Caleb eyed my phone as I opened the message. His mouth formed a straight line and he glanced down at his food. He seemed bothered.

From my messenger app, I sent a text to Sarah, letting her know I was coming back to East Greenwich today. We had kept in touch the last few weeks. What happened at the club had freaked her out, but she was ready to join me back in crime solving mode the moment I needed her again.

I looked back up at Caleb, who now stood next to me.

"Dorian and Noah are following Maurice for us. He tracked him down a few days ago," I explained. I waited for a response.

Nothing.

I cleared my throat and took a few more bites of breakfast. I couldn't handle the silence anymore. "They're helping us, Caleb. I think I may have spotted Maurice a few weeks back in Salem, but I wasn't sure. He didn't leave for the west coast like the rumors had indicated. He was here. Having Dorian and Noah on our team and helping us track him is a good thing."

He let out a subtle grunt, still chewing his last bite, and walked over to the sink, placing it inside and turning on the water to rinse it.

"I don't like him," he confessed as he turned around. "I never have. But I'm thankful he's willing to protect you and track Maurice for us."

I'm sure that took a lot of humility to admit, and that isn't something that comes easy for Caleb.

I studied his unreadable expression for a few seconds and said, "So, you won't mind if I have dinner with him tonight?"

His eyes widened, but he kept his cool. "Of course not."

I relaxed my shoulders.

That's a lie, but at least we aren't arguing over it.

I had to change the subject, or this was going to lead to awkwardness, and I was too tired for that. "Was your date with Melissa last night?"

His mouth curved into a smile. "Actually, yes. We went to La Masseria. We had a nice time. She's sweet."

Sweet? He avoided saying "beautiful." She was definitely beautiful, and I knew he thought that. He needed to understand that I didn't care.

"That's great," I said before taking a few more sips of my coffee. "Mind if I use your shower to get ready? I don't need the twenty questions at my house with the coven. I'll call them to let them know I'm back in town, but I have too many things to catch up on now that I'm home."

"Of course. Clean towels are in the hallway closet. Roland gets back from his trip today, and I'll let him know about the possibility that this could be Maurice."

"When do Abigail and Desiree get back from Hawaii?"

"*If* they come back." He smirked. "It's been a while since they've been in the sun."

I smiled at that thought. Abigail and Desiree were the first vampires who stepped up to be changed back to their human form. They weren't just human again, they had their powers back, which they had always yearned to have again. They never loved what they were, just like Dorian, though I couldn't see him changing his mind any time soon.

Caleb pulled me out of my thoughts by walking up to me and placing his hand on my fingers. He didn't grab my hand, but his touch lingered on my skin, ever so delicately. "Have a nice date with Dorian tonight."

He smiled and walked away. I could have explained to him that Dorian and I weren't dating, but I knew it was pointless. He had only said that to get under my skin.

Caleb was Caleb again.

———

I visited Lily for an hour, then stopped by Laurie and Cami's to take care of a few household chores. I finished the rest of the day by getting groceries, since I had been gone for three weeks, and met with Joel for a light lunch before I took off again to meet Dorian.

"Are you going to order food?" the same waitress from last time asked.

"Water and your cobb salad," I said.

She smiled and left us to put in our order.

It was nice seeing Dorian again. I did miss his company.

"Glad you're eating," he teased.

"You're one to talk. How *are* you surviving these days without the clan's supply?"

He looked away as if ashamed to tell me.

"You can tell me; I won't judge you unless you're killing people." I half-smiled and he didn't reciprocate.

"Noah, actually."

My mouth gaped open.

"He's strong enough to have me drink from him when I need to feed."

From the first time I met him, he never liked what he was. In the seventeenth century, we didn't have blood banks like we do today, and no one in their right mind would willingly give them their blood. I was too afraid the coven would find out, so I never offered him mine. If I did, he would have turned human, and he wouldn't be sitting here in front of me now. Dorian had to take blood against people's will back then, but he was weirdly polite about it, always apologized, and practically starved himself to death until he absolutely needed to eat to survive.

After being rescued from Maurice's clan, and before we went our separate ways, he explained how Maurice would let him drink the drained blood from those hooked up to the tank, who had tried to run. Maurice would have kicked him out for not blending in with the other clan members, but Dorian offered up his services to be one of his bodyguards in exchange for Dorian never having to pierce the skin of another victim. He had chosen not to own a human or witch and did his best to stay as invisible as possible.

"How does that work exactly? He isn't human."

"On the contrary. His DNA *is* human. He was born a shapeshifter, yes, but when a shifter changes, their DNA changes. As long as I drink from him while he's in human form, I can survive on his blood," he explained. He looked up at our waitress as she set our drinks down on the table.

"Your salad will be right out," she said, smiling at Dorian. He smirked in her direction but shifted his gaze back to me almost immediately.

"How are you?" he asked.

His question took me aback. How was I? I don't even know how to answer that without lying or breaking down. I thought after everything I had been through since I found out my purpose here, I'd grown to handle *most* things, but finding out about my father being alive, Caleb finally letting me go, having Dorian back in my life after a year, and someone targeting innocents in order to get to me . . . again, was overwhelming me.

"I'm fine," I answered.

He narrowed his eyes at me and creased his brows. "Are you?"

"Look, Dorian, let's just stick to business."

"Business?" he asked in a tone which revealed how confused he was by my formality.

I can't do this.

"I just need to know about Maurice," I explained as I grabbed my salad bowl from the waitress the second she had handed it to me. "Thank you."

I dug my fork into my salad and took a bite as Dorian smirked at me. "He was last seen on Derby Street. He was meeting with a few of the guys I recognize from the old clan."

"Could you hear anything they were saying? Like, maybe why he's back in Massachusetts?" I asked after swallowing my bite.

"No, we didn't want to get too close, just in case they were listening, too."

I took another bite of my salad as a bell over the café doors chimed behind me. I turned around and spotted Noah walking in, in all his large and muscular glory.

"Is she all filled in?" he asked Dorian.

Dorian just nodded and tapped his fingers against the laminate table.

"Hi, Noah, nice to see you, too," I said.

Noah smiled at my remark and leaned back in his chair.

"How can we assist your coven?" Noah asked, holding his hands out and bowing.

I rolled my eyes and said, "If you could keep watching Maurice and report back to me or Caleb, I'd appreciate that." I looked over at Dorian. "Do you have Caleb's number? You don't always have to call me."

He snickered under his breath. "I'll just call you."

Noah shook his head at us and chuckled again. "Let's go, Dorian," he said, picking up his cell from the table. "I spotted Maurice about fifteen minutes ago in Salem."

"You fly fast," I said, remembering Noah in his eagle form the night he'd snatched me and took me to the lair.

"I guess you would know," Noah replied in a teasing manner. I crunched my face at him.

I didn't hate the guy, he was just doing his job back then, and it was me who'd sacrificed myself in the first place. He was always kind to me in the lair, and he was Dorian's best friend. So, if Dorian trusted him, so did I.

"I'll call you later." He scooted toward the edge of the booth until he and Noah stood next to me and looked down. "You look beautiful."

Those were the words he left me with, and I won't lie, it sounded nice coming from his lips.

CHAPTER FIFTEEN

Mercy

I'm no stranger to being followed. That was how this all began in the first place. I felt my skin prickle at the surface, while my heart pounded heavily against my chest. The leaves weren't crackling beneath their feet. Whoever was in the woods must have known better. They were careful, but I still knew they were there. Maybe it was my Spirit senses and gifts that Tatyana had given me when I was born.

I hurried into my house and secured the lock behind me. Leah and the boys were out getting milkshakes, according to her last text, so I would be alone until about ten tonight, unless they decided at the last minute to go somewhere else. I could have called Caleb, but did I really need him?

I locked all the windows and placed the box I had found at the doorstep on my kitchen counter. I stared at it for what felt like fifteen minutes before I grabbed a knife from the drawer and cut through the tape.

I pulled the flaps up and immediately stepped back.

Well, I didn't expect this.

Inside the box was a tightly-sealed glass mason jar of

what looked like blood. Folded around the jar with a rubber band was a small note.

My heart nearly exploded, and my jaw dropped. I've seen my share of blood, but this was different. I was being threatened in someone's sick game.

I should probably call Caleb, now.

I rang his line, but he didn't pick up.

Okay, I guess I'm calling Dorian.

He, however, did pick up. I explained to him what I had seen, and he agreed to come over.

He arrived at my house within twenty minutes, and my nerves had calmed down enough to where I had finally stopped pacing the floor.

I let him in and gestured to the box. "I haven't touched anything." I looked up at him. "Is this human blood?"

I wondered if he could smell it through a sealed mason jar.

He shook his head. "It's sealed airtight. I'll need to open it."

"No. Don't. What about fingerprints?" I asked.

"For one, if someone went to this length to send this to you, I guarantee they were wise enough to wear gloves. I would be careful about my own fingerprints, but you and I both know we aren't giving this over to the police."

Okay, he was right. This was a situation only *we* could handle. The last thing we wanted was for the police to put themselves in danger because it led them to a supernatural creature they didn't know how to take down. I walked over to the mason jar and grabbed the lid, gripped it tightly, and turned it until the sealed lid popped up, releasing the air inside. The strong aroma of copper and iron filled my senses, and I looked up at Dorian as his fangs protruded and his eyes turned as red as the liquid inside the jar. He backed up, composing himself, and let out the breath he had been holding in.

"Yeah, that's blood," he affirmed.

"Human?"

He nodded.

I grabbed the lid and sealed it back up. I placed it on the counter then pulled out the note from under it.

St. Mary's Cemetery. 9 P.M. Come Alone

I looked up at Dorian. "This may be the only way to catch who's doing this. I know it's crazy, but I need to go."

"You don't have to explain this to me. I'm not telling you to not go. I'll go with you, though, and stay hidden."

I nodded and eyed the clock. It was eight thirty.

"We have to go," I said.

I didn't have a plan. All I hoped for was that whoever was after me wouldn't be a coward tonight and that they would show themselves so I could take them out.

We drove to Saint Mary's Cemetery and parked a few blocks

down the road. Dorian hid behind a large grove of trees as I scanned the grounds. I didn't see or sense anyone.

"Come out, you coward!" I screamed. I held my hands out, energy radiating from the tips of my fingers.

I still didn't see any movement, but I did see an object a couple hundred yards in front of me. It was hard to see exactly what it was because it was dark now, and the cemetery wasn't lit up by street lights. I approached a large cement crypt, and my heart beat faster than it had ever done before when I was able to clearly see what was in front of me.

A rush of adrenaline coursed throughout my entire body as the world around me spun. I had to pace my breathing to slow down my pulse as my heart pounded hard against my chest, feeling like my chest was going to explode.

No . . . No! It can't be.

"Dorian?!" I yelled as I heard him speed up toward me. I felt the breeze from his movements caress my skin. He stopped and stared with me.

"Oh, no," he said.

"Is it really her?" I asked. I looked at him. "I don't understand. Where are her wings?"

"She's fallen," he explained, still staring at her. I didn't understand what he meant by "fallen."

I looked back to the crypt. Tatyana, the angel who had created me, was laying on her back across the crypt without her wings.

She looked human.

A sword pierced through her stomach, and blood was rolling down the cemented crypt onto the cemetery grounds.

I turned away from her, and my legs buckled underneath me, causing me to fall to the floor. I couldn't hold in the vomit that rose in my throat. After I stopped throwing up, I wiped my lips with my sleeve. I placed both my hands on the grass and dug my fingers deep into the soil while I gritted my teeth. I felt Dorian's hand on my shoulders, and I squeezed my eyes shut. After a few minutes, I turned to face him and held out my hand so he could pull me to my feet. Tears poured down my face as I looked back at her.

Someone had killed her. Why was she even here? And what the hell happened to her wings?

CHAPTER SIXTEEN

Mercy

The coven surrounded me as my hands trembled around a mug of tea. Leah rubbed my arm to try to calm me, but I couldn't relax. I couldn't get the image of Tatyana's body lying there with a sword through her stomach, covered in a pool of her own blood, out of my mind.

"She's in shock," I heard Dorian tell them, but I looked up toward Caleb.

They can't see me like this.

"She's dead," I stated for the twentieth time.

"We know," I heard Caleb say as he sat down next to me.

"How?" I asked, still not understanding what had happened. "She's not mortal. She's an angel."

I looked over at Dorian, who had his arms crossed over his chest. "She's fallen."

"What does that mean?" I asked.

"When she rescued me, she told me she couldn't come back. She was only allowed to create the Chosen Ones. She was never supposed to help you beyond that. She said if she ever came back, she'd have to sacrifice her wings and become mortal," Dorian explained. "She's a fallen angel."

I looked at Caleb and the rest of the coven. "But why would she do that? Why was she even here?" Dorian shrugged, so I looked over at Caleb. "Why would she sacrifice her wings?"

"I don't know, either, Mercy," Caleb said.

My hands gripped into fists as the only obvious explanation hit me. "Maurice. It has to be Maurice." I looked up. "She took down his clan to rescue everyone and took everything from him. Maybe she came to warn us about what he's been doing, and he killed her to stop her." I turned to Caleb again. "It *has* to be him."

Caleb placed his hand on mine and gripped it tightly. "Then we will find him and kill him."

The rest of the coven had been silent up until now. They joined him, agreeing with Maurice being the prime suspect in the murders in East Greenwich and of Tatyana, though Ezra brought up a good point. It could be two totally different killers. A vampire didn't kill Tatyana. It was death by sword, not by a bite.

The fury in the room from the coven gave me hope. I wasn't alone in my anger and desire to find him and make him pay for what he was doing. What he had done to Tatyana, to the innocent victims in East Greenwich, all of it. It had to end now.

"What do you want to do?" Caleb asked me.

"I want to *talk* to Maurice. We can't kill him just yet," I said, knowing they would never be okay with that.

"No." This time, Leah stepped up. "No way. It's too dangerous, and you know it."

"I'll go with her," Dorian said, stepping near me. "I know him."

"And you betrayed him. He'll kill you," Caleb added, but when he saw Dorian by my side and me not backing down, he said, "So the three of us will go."

"What do you want us to do?" Simon asked, moving toward Ezra and Leah.

"I'd love to kick a vampire's ass right about now. It's been awhile," Ezra added, pulling his lips into a grin.

"No one is kicking anyone's ass. I just need to talk to him and find out what he wants. My blood is of no use to him. He doesn't want to be human. Do you think he'd really risk his life over taking down his lair? He knows I can't be killed, unless..."

I paused, looking up at Caleb. "Caleb, when was the last time you checked on the dagger?"

"The dagger?" Leah squealed. "I thought Joel teleported it somewhere we weren't supposed to know about?"

Caleb turned to her. "Simon and I teleported to its location and retrieved it to protect Joel. He isn't strong enough to defend himself against a witch trying to read his mind. I have it hidden in Abigail's mansion."

Simon looked down and tried not to make eye contact with Leah and Ezra.

Leah gasped and Ezra threw his hands up. "Gee, that would have been nice to know since our entire lives depend on if someone finds it." His tone was full of both anger and panic. He turned to Simon. "I expected something like this from Caleb, but not you, man."

Simon shrugged.

"Enough!" I yelled. I was too exhausted for this. "Caleb, we need to go check on it. Now."

Dorian was still adamant about going with me to see Maurice, so it looked like Caleb, Dorian, and I were going on a little trip together after we made sure the dagger was exactly where Caleb had put it.

We climbed into Caleb's car and went to the mansion, walking up to the second floor and into Caleb's room. He lifted the floorboard, opened the safe, and cracked open the lid. And we just stared. I felt like all the air left my lungs, and I had to steady my breathing so I didn't pass out.

"Caleb, how could this happen?" I asked him, while keeping my eyes on the empty safe in front of us.

His mouth gaped open. He was just as in shock as me.

"Caleb?"

"Only a witch could have opened this," he finally answered.

"We are such fools," I added. When I felt someone's

touch, I looked down to see Dorian's hand wrapped around mine, gripping it firmly,

"He won't touch you," Dorian said. "I'll kill him myself."

Caleb narrowed his eyes down to where I was holding Dorian's hand, but I didn't care. I was angry at him for being so careless about hiding the dagger. I should have moved it somewhere safer the moment I found out it was *only* in a safe in the mansion.

"Let's go," I said to them both.

We drove toward Salem, where Noah had just reported having seen Maurice.

CHAPTER SEVENTEEN

Mercy

This new lair was much different than the gothic mansion he'd lived in before. There was no security gate. It almost looked normal. Almost *too* normal. This thought didn't sit well with me.

Noah reported that he had spotted Maurice coming in and out of this two-story Victorian-style home several times a week since he started to trail him. We guessed this was his home.

I could already feel my powers radiate inside me, but I had to take a few deep breaths to conceal it so I didn't lose control. My father taught me how to subdue my powers when I'd get upset, while I stayed with him those few weeks. We found that any time my emotions took over, so did my powers. We believed that it was due to not gradually getting used to them over the course of eighteen years, which is why witches didn't get all their powers at once. It was too overwhelming. The last year, I had not only learned what I was, but I'd gained all my powers *and* my mother's, all at once. I thought I had control, but it was evident that I didn't.

"We should just knock," I suggested. Dorian and Caleb

looked at me like I was crazy. "If we threaten him, he will attack."

They must have known I was right because they didn't argue.

We walked up to the door and knocked.

The feeling of butterflies fluttered in my stomach when Kyoko opened the door. She was quite loyal, I had to give her that.

"Well, well, well," she said. "Maurice?" She kept her eyes on me. "We sure have missed you. You have some guts coming here, but that's to be expected. You were always so careless, Mercy."

I didn't want to give her the impression that her words would faze or upset me, so I said nothing. She straightened out her pencil skirt and fidgeted with her fingers for a few seconds before we heard footsteps coming toward us. It was clear that I made her nervous, and that gave me great satisfaction.

"Dorian, looking handsome as ever," she added, right before Maurice stepped in front of me. My stomach churned, but I had to remind myself to be strong. The only thoughts going through my mind were the memories of every awful thing he had done to me a year ago.

Dorian grabbed my right hand, and Caleb gripped my left.

"Well, come on in, you three," Maurice said, not taking his eyes off mine. He gave a sinister smile as I walked past him, and it felt like a hard lump was pressing against my throat.

Dorian and Caleb stayed close to me while we walked in. I felt like I had two bodyguards I really didn't need. I wondered if the protection was for me or Maurice and Kyoko. They knew I was on the verge of ripping off their heads, but we couldn't take them out just yet.

Kyoko stood by the fireplace while Maurice adjusted his silk, collared shirt and glared at me as if he wanted to devour every part of my soul. This feeling caused my powers to ignite beneath my fingertips.

Relax, Mercy, or you're going to lose control.

"The dagger. Where is it?" I asked.

He chuckled and turned to Kyoko. "Did you take their precious little dagger?"

She shook her head and smirked. "No, Master. I did not."

Their behavior was strange, and it only made me more nervous to be here. As much as I wanted answers, I didn't want to be around these two.

Maurice didn't move closer to me, though I could see in his eyes he was ready to strike. He wouldn't while I had Caleb and Dorian on each side of me. I really wanted to kill this son of a bitch, but I needed answers.

"Cut the crap, Maurice. Where is it?" Caleb asked.

He laughed again but kept his eyes directly on me. "If I had the dagger, Mercy, I'd be using it to take out your coven."

I wasn't sure how to respond to that. Could it be someone

else? Maurice was too much of a narcissist to not admit how "amazing" he was for being one step ahead of us.

"The killings in East Greenwich? Is that you?"

He shook his head. "No. I don't need to kill human scum to get to you. I've been watching you ever since you left my lair. If I wanted you dead, I'd come for you."

My stomach twisted again. He was so sick.

"Tatyana?"

He stood there, non-responsive, then a slow grin formed on his face. "Oh, yes, that one *was* me."

I pounced on him like a lion after a gazelle. Green energy flew not just from my fingertips, but from my entire body. I tackled Maurice to the ground. Then, I heard a commotion behind me. I used my human strength and punched him straight in the face, drawing blood from his lip. I punched him harder and harder as I used my powers to pin him to the ground with my other hand. I wanted to kill him, to rip his head off. I could have easily killed him right then and there, if I wanted to, but I needed to know why. Why did he kill her?

I felt hands around my waist, then someone jerked me off him.

It was Dorian.

I looked back at Caleb, who had Kyoko in a chokehold. I knew it wouldn't be enough to subdue her for long, unless we plunged a stake through her heart, but it was enough to freeze her where she stood. For now.

Maurice stood in front of us, panting, his face covered in blood, while Dorian stood by my side.

"Why? Why did you kill her?" I asked, adrenaline still coursing through my veins.

Maurice laughed and glared at me with red eyes blazing. "I'd been following you for months, and just as I was about to take you again, the angel who destroyed everything I had, came to Salem looking for you. To my surprise, her wings were gone. I don't know why she was there, but I wasn't going to let her reach you. She had to pay for what she did."

My anger raged. "I hate you."

"Likewise, Akasha."

I cringed at the sound of the name he'd insisted on using a year ago. I hated that name and loathed the sound of it coming from his lips.

"Keep him on the ground. I'm going to look around for the dagger," Dorian said.

Caleb remained where he was, gripping Kyoko's arms and keeping her in place.

Maurice didn't take his eyes off me. The wounds from my bloodied fist had already healed, and Maurice wiped off his own blood with the bottom of his shirt.

Dorian came in a few minutes later, shaking his head. "I don't see it anywhere, but it doesn't mean it's not here."

Maurice laughed again. "Man, you three are something else. I don't have your dagger. As I said, I would have used it to kill the coven already." He glared back to me. "But not you, Mercy. I have other plans for you."

I gulped. I didn't like the sound of that. Not one bit.

Caleb released Kyoko but shoved her, causing her small frame to go flying forward.

I stepped toward Maurice, kicking him in the face one more time because I could. He was still on his knees, and I had all the power right now. If I wasn't ready to kill him, I was going to make him suffer just a little longer.

He was up to something, and knowing Maurice, he never worked alone. He wasn't smart enough to pull anything off without an army of followers.

"I have a stake, Mercy. You can use it on him right now," Caleb said.

I shook my head as he handed it to me. "Not yet. Not until we find out what he's hiding from us." I turned to Maurice. "What are you not telling us?

Maurice stayed silent.

I walked over to face Kyoko, her eyes widening. "Drink from my wrist or die, Kyoko."

Her eyes grew even wider, and she looked at Maurice as if she hoped he would save her, but he wouldn't move to her rescue. His eyes, however, were crimson red, and he showed his fangs, threatening me.

"Answer, Kyoko, or I'll answer for you," I threatened .

"I'd rather die than be a pathetic human," she said.

I stepped closer to her, and she didn't move, but Maurice did. He ran toward me with lightning speed, but Caleb lifted his hands and blasted a flame at him. It hit Maurice hard against the chest, and Dorian was by his side, holding him down.

"I'm sorry, but you and Maurice are too dangerous when you work together. But don't worry, Maurice will be joining you very soon in whatever dark hell you guys go to after this life."

"Oh, Akasha, if you only knew your fate. You think this is over, but it's not," she said. I knew it was a real threat. They had something planned.

"Goodbye, Kyoko," I said as I plunged the stake into her chest.

Maurice hissed behind me while trying to stand, but Dorian kicked him in the face so hard that this time, he blacked out. We knew it wouldn't be long before he regained consciousness, so we left as soon as I picked up the stake and handed it back to Caleb.

"Let's go."

CHAPTER EIGHTEEN

Mercy

Caleb left to meet up with Melissa. He was worried and wanted to check on her, especially now that we had pissed off Maurice enough that he would go after the ones we cared about.

Dorian and I stood outside my place when he dropped me off. The coven waited for me inside. "Can we talk for a minute?" he asked.

I nodded.

"I know this is really bad timing, but there's an art gallery show on Friday that I think you'd enjoy. I know Joel and Derek love art, maybe they'd like to come."

I wasn't sure what his angle was. Was he asking me on a date?

"When have you ever wanted to get to know Joel and Derek?" I asked, but he only frowned. "Dorian, what's going on?"

He looked away then back to me. "I needed a hobby when you left me," he confessed.

"*Your* party?"

I was surprised when he nodded. I had no idea he had an artistic side.

I smiled. "I'd love to go."

Thursday came and went, and by Friday, I was nervous for this gallery event. I hadn't done anything normal in a while, and going to a party with someone I used to love wasn't something I expected to happen, especially with everything going on—the murders, the dagger missing, and Maurice threatening us. There was so much going on right now that needed the coven's attention to protect those around us, I almost felt guilty going out and having fun.

Dorian and I arrived at the gallery event around seven in the evening. A waitress walked by with a serving tray of wine and I grabbed one before she could pass me.

I felt more nervous tonight than I had in a while. I thought maybe the wine would help me relax a bit. So much had gone on this last week, and I couldn't shake the thought that Maurice was going to strike after what I did to Kyoko. There was also that feeling we all had that he was up to something, and whatever plan that was, it was about to hit us straight on.

"Mercy, I don't like telling you what to do, but I know what the alcohol can do to your powers, so maybe just one drink? Just in case," he whispered in my ear. The heat from his breath near my skin created goosebumps on my neck.

What the hell?

"I just need to relax," I confessed. I wasn't sure if this nervous feeling was because Maurice could bust down these doors at any minute, or because I was here with Dorian. Someone I loved years ago. I had to remind myself that if it was the latter, it was just physical attraction.

"Are you nervous about something?" he asked with a small smirk that pulled at the side of his mouth.

I rolled my eyes, not wanting to entertain his assumptions, and looked around the gallery. My mouth gaped open as I saw the paintings around me. They were breathtaking . . . and familiar.

I padded across the gallery toward a painting of a woman's face, painted in dark amber, green, and yellow. It was a face that reflected my own. I turned toward the others, and they were all of our old village in Salem. He had painted images of old buildings from my visions. There were paintings of children in Puritan clothing playing in a field.

They were all so beautiful, but also sad. He had created a world that was no longer mine, no longer ours. But why?

I turned to him. "Why did you paint these?"

He smiled while taking a sip of the white wine from his glass. "It was the last time I was truly happy—when I had you as mine."

How do I respond to this?

"See, Joel, why are we not opening a gallery here? Look how many guests have shown up," I heard Derek ask. I felt instant relief they were here.

"True. I just wasn't sure how long we'd be here to even think about opening another gallery," Joel responded, grabbing a wine glass from the tray as the same waitress walked by.

"Grab two," I said.

Joel raised an eyebrow.

"I'm nervous, Joel. After what we did to Kyoko . . ."

"You had to. You know that," Joel said.

"I know, but he'll be out for blood now."

Joel rolled his eyes. "More reason to *not* drink." He grabbed my half-empty glass and placed it on the table next to me.

The party had died down around ten, so Dorian grabbed my jacket from the coat closet and locked up.

I heard a text come through as I climbed into Dorian's car. Lily and Bradley wanted to host a breakfast tomorrow morning at her place with just the family. They had something to talk to us about.

Dorian drove me home and leaned in, gently kissing my cheek. "Thank you for coming tonight. It meant a lot to me."

"How did you do tonight? Did you sell any paintings?"

He smiled. "I sold about eight and grabbed a few business cards, but truthfully, I don't do it for the money. Just having the paintings there for people to look at, and for me to see them on display, is all that matters."

I placed my hand on his and tilted my head. "I'm sorry you feel like you can't be truly happy anymore."

He turned his palm up and squeezed my hand. "I am happy."

I hope so.

"Goodnight, Dorian." And I kissed him gently on the cheek.

CHAPTER NINETEEN

Caleb

Melissa's hands trembled. I reached out and caressed them with my fingertips, hoping to steady her aim. "Now pull it back and let go," I instructed.

She steadied the bow and let go. The arrow flew toward the target and hit the tree a few inches from the center. "Yes! Was that good? I think it was good. I mean, for a rookie, right?"

She's so adorable.

"That was great. We can practice out here any time you'd like. I know you hate guns, so learning archery is a great alternative."

She laughed. "Are you trying to turn me into a super-hero? I'm not like you guys."

I brushed the hair from her face. "No, but it's dangerous to be unarmed."

"I have mace. I mean, really, Caleb, you think I'm going to carry a bow and arrow every time I walk alone?"

I laughed. It was silly. She needed something practical she could always have with her, but watching her shoot an arrow toward a tree was the highlight of my morning. She looked so sexy doing it. "I can show you how to throw a knife. You can keep a dagger in your purse."

She nodded. "That's more like it. You can teach me during our next session, Sensei," she teased, bringing her palms together and bowing.

I leaned closer to her, placed my hands around her neck, and pulled her to me. Her lips met mine, passionately and seductively. She was going to drive me crazy, but I wouldn't have it any other way.

Her fingers lingered on the back of my head, and she gripped my hair lightly.

"Caleb, I . . ." I didn't know what she wanted to say to me, but she looked as if she was battling something in her mind. "I have to get back to the office."

I knew that wasn't what she wanted to say, but I didn't press her.

"You also have your training, right?"

I nodded. "Yeah, they're on their way. It's easier for us to practice the magic part of our defense outside of the basement. Just in case it gets out of hand." I laughed and she shook her head at me.

"You're crazy," she said as she leaned in to kiss me.

***

Shortly after she left, the rest of the coven showed up, except for Mercy, who had something to do at her aunt's house this morning.

"I like this spot. It's more secluded here," Leah said as she neared the clearing.

I had cleared an open area of forest debris and stood at the center before Leah, Simon, and Ezra joined me.

We joined hands, formed a circle, closed our eyes, and chanted a spell we had been working on. I felt my powers flow through me, and when we opened our eyes, they were glowing a bright shade that represented our elements.

Leah lifted her hands and pulled the water from the soil around us. It had rained earlier, so she was able to extract enough to form a large pool of water in her palms.

"Okay, you can use me. Go for it," Ezra said, just seconds before Leah threw the water ball at him and encased his head, drowning him with her powers. He pulled his hands up to his neck and gasped for air. She released the water back down to the earth, and Ezra coughed up the remaining liquid that had entered his lungs. "Man, I love your power," he said.

I chuckled at the two of them and turned to Simon. "Your turn."

Simon lifted his hands and a gentle breeze tickled my neck. The force of the breeze picked up, along with the leaves around us, blowing violently like a hurricane passing by. As the wind encircled the coven, I felt the air leave my lungs and I couldn't breathe. The air encircled us like a tornado, and Leah had to brace herself on the ground, gripping a branch in order to keep from flying away. I became lightheaded, and Ezra's hand raised, signaling it was enough, so Simon lowered his hands, and we all gasped for air, pulling it back into our lungs so we could breathe again.

Ezra turned to me. "I'm . . . next," he said, still trying to catch his breath.

Leah and Simon smiled at him and grabbed a branch next to them.

Ezra shook his head. "Yeah, that isn't going to save you."

Ezra's hands raised, and I heard the ripping of the roots from the trees around us as he pulled branches in our direction. He threw his hands out, and a branch flew toward Simon, grabbing him by the foot and pulling him away from the branch he held on to. Ezra directed the branch, which Simon had thought was his saving grace, to wrap around Simon's wrist and the two branches stretched his body out until he could no longer move.

Leah decided to run, which wasn't the best move. Ezra used his powers to pull the soil up from the ground, which created a hole which Leah fell into.

I pulled my arms out to the sides, fireballs appeared at my fingertips, and I threw them toward Ezra, but he had powered up the leaves on the ground in front of him to create a wall for protection. The fireball slammed into it and burned the leaves instead.

I held up a hand, Ezra released his power, which was still holding onto Simon, and I walked over to Leah to help her out of the hole.

"Okay, I think this was the most fun we have had in a while. Can we please do this more often?" Leah asked as she gripped my hand.

"I do love the sparring though," Simon added.

"The sparring is needed to take out a vampire, guys," I told them. "There may be a situation where our powers are taken from us, like they were with Mercy when she was held captive in the lair. By us knowing how to kickbox and having the ability to take out a vampire with our hands and not our powers, we will fight so much better. Trust me."

"Yeah, we get it, but this was so much more fun." Ezra beamed.

I looked up at the sky and grey clouds were forming overhead. "A storm is supposed to roll in today. We can keep practicing or head out."

"We'll keep training," Leah answered for everyone.

Simon and Ezra both nodded.

We trained for another hour, but when the storm became too fierce, we headed back. It was true that with Ezra's power, he controlled the elements of earth, which meant he could control the weather, but we vowed to let nature take its course and only use our magic if it was necessary or when we were training.

CHAPTER TWENTY

Mercy

It was early, and I mean early. I eyed the clock as I neared Lily's home, and it read eight in the morning.

On a Saturday.

Why do people do this?

I walked in and found Lily in the kitchen, cooking our breakfast. Bradley was setting the table and smiled at me when I walked in. Joel was sitting on the couch, watching the morning news, and I didn't see Derek anywhere.

"Where's Derek?" I asked as I joined him on the couch.

"New York."

I cocked an eyebrow.

"He's meeting with an art collector and a real estate agent this weekend," he explained.

"Are you moving here permanently?" I asked, my voice raising.

That would be awesome to have him so close.

He smiled and turned off the TV, directing his attention back to me. "We are. We're going to list our home in two weeks," he said.

I beamed! "Joel, that's amazing news." I looked over at

Lily in the kitchen. "Is that why everyone is meeting here? To tell me that?"

He shook his head. "No, the news is something Lily wants to share with us. I still don't even know."

"Breakfast is ready," Lily called from the kitchen.

We sauntered into the kitchen and took our seats.

Lily had made pancakes with chocolate and fruit toppings. I loved these pancakes. She also didn't eat dairy or eggs, so she'd found this vegan recipe years ago with my mom and we'd eat this during the holidays or on the occasional Sunday morning family get-togethers.

I dove in, forking the corner of my pancake, not adding any toppings to it, yet. "What's the big news you wanted to share?" I asked, my mouth stuffed.

She looked at Bradley, who had a huge grin on his face, then held out her hand. A bright, shiny diamond ring almost blinded me.

I looked back up and Joel looked just as shocked as me.

"Congratulations, guys," I said.

I was happy for them, but I was also nervous. We barely knew him, and what did that mean for our secret? Joel had never told Derek about us being witches, but once, he had walked in on Joel performing a spell when Joel wasn't expecting him home. They had already been married for a few years but had dated since they were in high school. We loved Derek. We trusted him, and to this day, he's never told anyone, and he accepted that part of our lives.

Of course, at the time, I didn't even know what I was, and

he kept the family secret like Lily and Joel had, to protect me.

Maybe Bradley was like that, too, but I'd been so busy with this newfound discovery of who I was that I hadn't been able to get to know him like I should have by now.

"Thank you," Lily said.

Bradley squeezed her hand. "We aren't getting married right away," he added. "Don't worry. We're setting the wedding date for next spring."

This made me feel a bit better.

We finished our food and cleaned the dishes. Bradley and Joel stepped into the family room to watch something on the TV, and I helped Lily in the kitchen.

"Does he know about us? Or do you plan to tell him?" I asked her.

She placed the last plate in the dishwasher and turned around to face me. She leaned her back against the counter and wrapped her arms around her waist. "I want to tell him. I brought it up to Caleb the other day. It won't be easy to keep quiet the fact that you and Joel aren't witches and yet I am. We're from the same bloodline. Not that people who don't know about us would put something like that together, but he might."

I nodded. "I get it. You can tell him I'm a witch, but, of course, ask Joel about his secret. I just think telling him about the whole vampire thing may be a bit overwhelming for him."

She chuckled. "Yeah, he may not take that so well."

I smiled. "Tell him, but know that it could put his life in

danger the more he knows."

"I thought about that," she said. "The whole 'keeping a secret from your loved ones in order to keep them safe.'" She looked down and bit her lower lip. "But it didn't keep Cami safe."

That stung. Not that Lily blamed me, though I sure blamed myself, but she was right. Cami didn't know about us, and yet, she had been taken over by the darkest of evil. I didn't protect her.

I was now thinking about Cami being locked away inside the Asylum, all alone and terrified about what was happening to her. There was no way for her to escape her nightmare. "I should go visit her today," I said.

"Want me to go with you?" she asked.

I shook my head. "Thanks, though." I leaned into the family room. "Congrats again, Bradley." His eyes stayed glued to the TV. "Joel, I'm heading to Salem to see Cami. I'll catch up with you later."

They just threw a hand up in the air to send me off with a wave, and that was good enough.

Mr. Kriser handed me my badge and escorted me to the same room where my mom had died in my arms. A rush of emotions hit me as I neared that door that led into the room that changed my entire life.

My mom didn't just die in there, I killed her. Her lifeless

body had laid heavily in my arms, her eyes still open, watching me. I don't know how long after someone had died that their spirit lingered in or above them, but I felt my mom watching me cry. I would never get that feeling out of my mind.

I probably should have gone through therapy after what happened, but I went from my mom dying, to my Awakening, to bringing down Maurice's lair, to having to train daily to be this vampire hunter that I was destined to be. I couldn't mourn like normal people. There was nothing I could even do to heal my mind. I had to live in the nightmare, no matter how hard it was for me. I didn't have a choice.

"I don't know if I can do this," I admitted as he gestured for me to enter the room.

He looked at the cracked-open door and back at me. "I can see if the break room is available."

I shook my head. "No, I can do this. Sorry." I stared at the door intently. "Just give me a minute."

I closed my eyes and took a deep breath, hoping it would calm my nerves. After a few slow breaths, it worked. I felt my body relax, but it wasn't just this room that made me nervous. This hospital masked our powers. I still had them, of course, but there was that shield that protected the staff from the creatures behind these walls, keeping me from using them. This was the first time in a year I felt normal. It was both refreshing and terrifying.

I entered the room. Cami sat on a couch with her legs tucked under her. She didn't have her cell phone with her;

they wouldn't let the patients use them in here. She held a book instead. That was progress. Cami used to read all the time before her possession.

"What are you reading?" I asked as I sat down next to her. The sleeve from the book was missing, so when she didn't respond, I leaned forward, looking at the page, but it was upside down. She kept her eyes glued on the book and even flipped a page, scanning the words from top to bottom.

Great.

"Mercy," Doctor Harrison said as he entered the rec room. He was the therapist that had been working with my mom. Leah had assigned him to Cami's case as he was a witch who would, at times, perform an exorcism or a spell to help people who were once normal, but went insane, whether it was from true mental illness or if it was caused by an evil entity.

Leah had explained that they referred to him as a Witch Doctor or Shaman. He had the ability to not only connect with someone's spirit if they were still alive but could communicate with spirits who had passed on after this life and wanted to speak with the living. The only spirits he couldn't connect with were vampires.

He had asked me several times in the past if I wanted to reach out to my mother after she died, but I refused. I was too ashamed of what I had done, and I couldn't face what she'd say to me. Did she hate me for what I did? Worse than she already had?

I stood to my feet, shook his hand, and looked at Cami.

"I'll be right back."

She ignored me, still staring at the upside-down book as if she were reading.

"She's been like that since she arrived," Doctor Harrison explained as we entered the hall.

"She hasn't spoken?"

He shook his head. "Not a word."

This was disturbing. She at least spoke to me on occasion. It was always short and brief, but she still used her voice. Maybe she was scared and didn't trust anyone here. What if she was shutting down?

Doctor Harrison escorted me into his office and gestured for me to sit. He grabbed a folder and a recording device.

"When she first came here," he started, "I felt her energy, even inside these walls."

I held up my hand. "Wait, are you allowed to share this with me?"

It was a silly question. This wasn't a normal facility, and her mom wasn't in her right mind to make decisions for her, but there was still the issue of doctor-patient confidentiality.

"I know what you're thinking," he continued. "I *can* share her medical diagnosis with you. Laurie signed a consent form to allow us to speak with you on Cami's behalf."

I was happy to learn this. The more I knew, the more I could help her. *If* I could help her.

He pressed play on the audio device in front of him. I heard Doctor Harrison ask Cami a few questions about how she was feeling, then Cami screamed. She screamed so loudly that Doctor Harrison fumbled with the device to turn it down.

"Sorry," he said.

The scream faded, and she began mumbling gibberish. The words made no sense, as if she were speaking in tongues.

"What is she saying?" I asked.

He shook his head. "Nothing I've ever heard." He turned off the recording device and opened the binder in front of him. "I performed a spell to reach her mind. I needed to see what *she's* seeing." He placed the notebook back down. "Mercy, Cami is gone."

I wasn't sure if I had heard him correctly. "I don't understand."

"When I performed the spell, I saw through her eyes, but not what she's seeing in this world. I saw much deeper than that," he explained. My stomach dropped so far down, it felt as if it hit the floor. I could only imagine the worst—the nightmares that kept her up at night.

"Tell me."

He cupped his hands together and leaned back in his chair. "She's seeing hell."

This stunned me into silence. I couldn't breathe for a second until he said my name, pulling me back to him.

"Mercy, when Kylan's ghost entered her body, she saw every memory he had. Kylan may have lived on this earth, but he had access to a dark underworld where only the evilest of creatures ever go. He came and went between both worlds for centuries. I don't think it's the same type of hell you read about in the Bible. This is something else. When Kylan died, he left a part of him still dwelling and torturing her. The entity inside of Cami is killing her. Her mind is already gone, so she won't come out of this."

Tears welled in my eyes, and I let out a sob. "I'm sorry. I'm still not understanding. She's gone? Kylan is where?"

My mind was moving a million miles an hour.

I thought after she awoke from her spell, she'd be okay. Maybe she'd feel off for a bit, but she would come out of it, and we'd be goofing off at Goddard Park or having a deep conversation about a new guy she had met. But what he was telling me was that my best friend was dead and somehow still walking around like she'd been turned into a zombie-like creature. And Kylan was what? Still possessing her?

He grabbed a tissue from a box on the table and handed it to me, but I simply rubbed my eyes and put on a brave face. "Do I need to kill her to set her free?" My question came out cold and emotionless, but I didn't feel that way. I was torn up inside, but I couldn't let him see me that way. He was a witch that relied on me to protect them. I couldn't show this side of me.

I wouldn't.

He nodded. "Yes, Mercy. It's the only way to set her free so her spirt can move on to whatever life is after this. Her mind is gone, her body is weak, and her spirit is trapped. Kylan never left, and the only way to free Cami is to kill the body." He winced at his own words.

He sat up straight and continued. "Kylan was never like the vampires he created. He had a demonic spirit, whereas vampires have none. He is still possessing her, Mercy."

"Can we perform an exorcism to get him out of her and save what is left of Cami?" I asked.

He shook his head. "Even if we did an exorcism to remove Kylan's spirit, her mind is already gone. Her spirit was barely holding on before she came here. Kylan's power was so strong, the memories she's seeing will never truly go away. She will always be in that hell."

I stood up and turned to hide the emotions I wore on my face while trying my best to conceal the shaking going on inside me from the anger at what Kylan had done to her. I wasn't going to let him see how upset I was at myself for allowing it to happen in the first place.

"Okay. I'll do it," I said when I turned back around to look at him. "Do you need to lower the shield? I don't feel my powers."

He shook his head. "No. There is a room here that isn't protected. We will do it there."

I nodded and walked toward the door. "Well, let's get on with it."

I acted like a freaking robot to mask my feelings. Didn't I have to in order to kill one of my best friends?

No. Cami is already gone, I had to remind myself. Kylan killed her. I was simply setting what was left of her free. Right?

I walked down a long corridor that led to this other

room, while the doctor went to get her. Once I entered the room, I immediately felt my powers coming back into my body, and I sighed with relief.

I sat on a couch inside the room, looking around. The room was simple, aside from herbs and books that lined the walls. A chair with shackles sat in the middle of the room.

Oh, dear God. This must be where they do exorcisms.

Doctor Harrison entered the room, Cami's arm linked with his, and directed her to the chair.

"Please don't shackle her," I said.

A giggle escaped from Cami.

I walked up to her as her head hung low, staring at the floor. When her head popped up, I saw a look I hadn't seen from her this past year.

She grinned.

She didn't just grin, the corners of her mouth stretched so far that her lips reached the top of her cheek bones and her bottom lip ripped.

Oh, shit.

This wasn't Cami.

She giggled again and looked over at me. "Really? Is this what it's come down to?"

Okay, this is creepy.

"Um, Cami, why don't you have a seat, okay?" I said.

"Oh, goody!" Her voice sure didn't sound like Cami. She clapped her hands and still wore that stretched out, creepy grin.

She looked up at the doctor, and her face changed again,

but this time, her lips formed a flat line and her eyes narrowed, her brows tilting inward.

Was this Cami or Kylan looking at him? The face she wore was one I didn't recognize.

The doctor approached her, but he didn't get far. Her hand reached out, and without touching him, she flicked her wrist and his neck snapped. I gasped as his body collapsed to the floor.

"Cami, don't!" I screamed.

Her hand came up again, but when she did it with me, she grabbed my throat and squeezed so tight, I thought she'd crush my bones. I pulled my hands up and blasted her with my power across the room, but she hopped up the moment she hit the floor. She turned to face the wall, digging her fingers into the drywall . . . then climbed.

Oh, hell no.

She climbed like a demon-possessed vessel, scaled the walls, gripping it with the tips of her fingers as her body contorted in an unnatural position that made my skin crawl.

Soon, she was above me, and her neck twisted until she met my gaze and she laughed, but the tone of her voice was low and demonic.

She darted toward the window in the corner and slammed her fist against it, shattering the glass, and jumped out.

What. The. Hell. Was. That?

CHAPTER TWENTY ONE

Caleb

I sat on Mercy's bed with a note in my hand with her name on it. A note I had found under the doormat, waiting for her.

"I spoke with Leah," Ezra said when he entered the room. "Mercy was supposed to visit Cami at the hospital today. She's calling now to check on her."

I looked down at the note when Simon came in the room to join us. "Let's open it," Simon said. "It's not like it's a love note from a secret admirer. We know who it's from."

Mercy wasn't here, and this involved all of us. Addressed to her or not, I opened it.

I Have The Dagger

That was it. No one had signed it, and it didn't give instructions on what they wanted us to do or what their next play would be.

"What the hell am I supposed to do with this information?" I asked them.

"Whoever this is just wants to scare us. I mean, seriously,

if they have the dagger, why don't they just come after us?" Ezra asked.

Was this an empty threat? Or was this person stupid enough to come after the coven?

Maurice was the obvious choice, though I found it strange he wouldn't admit he was the killer when we cornered him. It wasn't like he was afraid of us.

Leah rushed into the room, panic reflecting in her eyes. "Raven's called. Cami escaped when Mercy was there."

"What?" I asked.

I looked at Simon and Ezra right as my phone beeped at my hip.

It was Mercy.

Mercy: *Cami's possessed by Kylan's spirit. Her mind is gone, and we can't bring her back. She escaped Raven's twenty minutes ago. We have to kill her, Caleb. Keep watch. I'm going to stay with Riley for a few days. Call or text if you need me, but I won't be coming home today.*

I didn't tell her about the note. As much as she needed to come home right now, she also needed to work out whatever was going through her head before she could face whoever was about to come for us, and we knew something or someone was coming.

"I'll call Joel and Lily," I said. "We need everyone paying attention right now. Between whoever has the dagger, Maurice's threat, and now Cami, I don't want us to be surprised when something happens, and I have a feeling something bad is about to happen."

I informed Lily and Joel of the latest developments and sent a few text messages to Riley, but he hadn't responded. I trusted him to be alone with her, but I needed to make sure he'd report to me when she wouldn't. Mercy being away from the coven again wasn't the best idea, but she needed him, and he was her best friend.

CHAPTER TWENTY TWO

Mercy

Riley's hand rested on my shoulder as he took a seat on the bench next to me. The last time we were at Goddard Park together was the day I had been released from the hospital. The day Caleb came back into my life.

"Is she really gone?" he asked, and I nodded. A tear formed in the corner of my eye and slowly trickled down.

He grabbed my hand and squeezed. I wiped away the tear and looked at him. "There's nothing left of her."

Now Riley's eyes watered, but he choked back his sobs. "Then you have to do it. You have to set her free."

I rested my head on Riley's shoulder and closed my eyes. His hand touched the top of my head, and he rubbed my hair like he was comforting a sick child. Riley was what I needed right now. With Riley, I wasn't afraid to show the weakest and most vulnerable parts of who I was. I could be me. He was my best friend and the one person who would listen to me without judgement.

We sat out there for what felt like hours. The wind picked up, and the breeze tickled my skin. He rubbed my arm gently, warming it up, and kissed me on the top of the head. It wasn't a romantic kiss. We cared about each other, and he was showing me that he understood the pain I felt because he felt it, too.

"Does the coven know where you are?" he asked. "Caleb has been reaching out to me."

I nodded and leaned back on the bench and continued to stare at the cove. "They know I'm fine."

"You're not fine," he said quickly. "None of us are."

My eyes stayed glued to the water. "I don't care anymore, Riley." The sun beamed down on my cheeks, warming them as we continued to sit on the bench, staring out at the lake.

I may have gained the knowledge of who I was in my past life and my purpose here. I had gotten my powers back, and this was supposed to be the new me, but why didn't it feel like it? I lost a huge part of who I was, and it all started the night my mom thought she had the right to snuff out my life.

Who am I, really?

I stood and walked to the edge where the grass met the water and cried harder than I had in years. My chest ached, and I found it hard to breathe. I slowly sucked in a breath, and when I released the air from my lungs, I rubbed the heel of my palm against my chest and clutched my jet stone necklace.

I felt the power inside me build, and I didn't care if a hiker or someone in their boat saw me or my power.

Then . . . I screamed.

I screamed so loudly that my chest ached, so I held my

hands against my chest, keeping them secure, but the energy was too much for me to conceal. My arms flew out and my powers left my fingertips, blasting across the park on each side of me. I heard trees timbering over and the water crashing in heavy waves. The noise was so powerful, it sounded like thunder crashing down from above us.

I relaxed just enough to pull back my power before I turned around to face Riley, who was standing there in his beautiful and glorious wolf form. Once we both met each other's gaze, his head flew up, and his snout pointed to the sky. His howl echoed through the woods around us, and the hairs on the back of my neck stood straight. It was the most beautiful sound I had ever heard.

I neared him slowly, and he bowed his head, so I dropped to my knees to be on his level, pressed my forehead to his, and let out the remaining breath I had held in. "Thank you," I whispered. "Thank you, Riley."

CHAPTER TWENTY THREE

Caleb

Sunday morning, as I crawled out of bed, I received a text from Riley saying he was still with Mercy. If she needed an escape, I'd give it to her. She had just learned she had to kill Cami, and I couldn't imagine what that felt like.

I didn't expect her to come to me for support. I couldn't replace what she and Riley had. None of us could.

I heard a knock at the front door. It was Melissa.

"Come on in," I said.

"I brought wine." She smiled and placed it on the table. "I'm sure it won't compare to what Abigail makes, but it's my favorite."

I leaned in, kissing her gently on the lips, and she welcomed my kiss. She looked nervous, and I didn't want her to feel this way around me.

I grabbed our dinner from the kitchen, and after we ate, I took her to the library, which was my favorite room in the house.

"There are so many books. I wish I had the time to read,

but my work keeps me busy, and by the time I'm home, I'm exhausted."

I smiled, turned toward her, and tucked her hair behind her ear. "Well, I'm glad you had time to spend with me tonight."

She tried to look down, but I wouldn't let her. I placed the tip of my finger on her chin and lifted it. I hated that this gesture made me think of Mercy. I couldn't think of her when I was with Melissa. I cared so much about this girl in front of me, I couldn't risk losing her, too.

"You're adorable. You know that?" I asked.

She chuckled. "I'm covered in tattoos. I don't know if 'adorable' suits me."

"Okay, then. You're sexy. You're so incredibly sexy."

She lifted on her tippy toes to reach my lips and kissed me. "Thanks. You're not so bad yourself," she said, followed by a wink. She looked around the library. "Which of these have you read?"

"Most of them."

"Most of them?" She gasped. "Seriously, there's easily over four-hundred books on these shelves."

I smirked. "I had these brought down from my place in Salem. I kept a few books I had read throughout the years, but I had to move around so much, I had to donate most of them. I didn't have the space at my place in Salem, and these shelves were empty. Abigail said I could keep them here."

"That's amazing." She scanned the shelves, trailing her fingers along the wood and wiping off the dust from her fingers when she reached the end. "You really have seen a lot, haven't you?"

I nodded. "Yes, but it also has been lonely," I confessed. "When you know you have all the time in the world, you waste it. You also keep to yourself because you'll just watch those you love die."

The words came out before I could stop them. Her face grew somber, but she didn't look away. "Then what are you doing with me?" she asked. I didn't have the answer to that. I wish I did. I'd tell her that I wanted her now. I wanted her tomorrow, and it didn't matter if she grew old and I didn't. It wouldn't matter if I watched her die at forty, sixty, or a hundred years old. I wanted to be with her.

"I want you, Melissa. I want you, not because I'm lonely, but because I care about you. Yes, Mercy took away whatever we had centuries ago. But I've let her go. I want *you*."

She placed her hand on my cheek. "Then why are we inside a library?"

I smiled, grabbed her hand, and escorted her upstairs. When we reached my bedroom, I turned her around to look at me, but I didn't say anything. I just unbuttoned her shirt and pulled it off her shoulders to reveal a sexy, pink-laced bra. I leaned down and kissed her passionately, pressing her closer to my body. I felt her hands at my waistline, undoing my buckle then pulling down my pants.

I pulled my t-shirt over my head and finished taking off my pants and boxers. I lowered her onto the bed, removing the rest of her clothes and tossing them on the floor. I kissed her on the lips and trailed my tongue to her neckline. She arched when my mouth touched her collarbone. As she lowered her hips, I steadied my knees on the bed, lifting just enough to take in her perfect body and the most intricate display of tattoos I had ever seen. Her body showed marks of art and stories from her life, and it was so goddamn sexy.

"Are you sure you want to do this?" I asked, then silently cursed at myself. Why was I asking her this right now? Of course she had wanted it. I guess I was just nervous. I *had* been with other women since I had been with Mercy in her previous life. But I didn't care for them like I had Mercy. No one had ever compared to her, so I gave my body to them but not my heart. They were just a way to pass the time until I brought her back. I didn't know if I was ever going to be able to bring Mercy back into this life, and I was lonely. With Melissa, it was different. I cared about her. I wasn't sure if it was love, but I cared for her more than I had anyone aside from Mercy.

She laughed. "Oh, boy. Are you really asking me this? Would I be lying here naked if I wasn't sure?"

I smiled and leaned down, kissing her on the neck and running my hands down her waist. I felt her skin ripple at the surface as I created goosebumps down her body. She moaned and placed her hands on the back of my head and fisted my hair, squeezing tightly until I moaned with her.

She released my hair when I removed my lips from her neck and smiled at me. "I love you, Caleb."

I stopped for a moment at those words. I wasn't sure

what I felt when it came to love. I couldn't say it back, but I didn't want her to feel embarrassed for not telling her that I did, too, so I leaned in and kissed her again, deepening the kiss until her moans turned me inside out.

I pulled myself up to look at her beautiful gaze one more time before our bodies became one. Her movements swayed with mine, and she breathed heavily at every touch.

Was this love? Not yet. But in this moment, she was everything. Everything I wanted, everything I needed, and I didn't want it to end.

The sound of broken glass echoed from the first floor. I sat bolt upright and looked over at Melissa, who was sound asleep. We crashed last night, and I never set the house alarm. Someone was inside the house.

I hurried downstairs, looking through every corner and room on the main level. Once I entered the library, I saw shards of glass on the ground below the window.

"You've picked the wrong house, buddy. I'd leave if I were you!" I shouted, right as a force hit the back of my head. I stumbled forward, but I was conscious enough to stay on my feet.

The intruder wore all black from head to toe, but the shape of his broad shoulders and thick, tall legs told me it was a man. Mask, gloves, and in one of his hands, a dagger.

Our dagger.

I lifted my hands and flames appeared. He charged toward me, but I moved left and slammed my elbow on the bridge of his back. He fell flat to his knees and dropped the dagger.

While he knelt on the wooden floor, I grabbed the dagger, but something burned my hand, so I quickly dropped it.

Dammit. Someone had laced it with magic. Whatever vampire this was, they were working with a witch.

Maurice.

"Get up, Maurice. I know it's you." He stood, and I mustered up the flames in both my hands. "You're not going to win this fight," I threatened, then blasted the flames toward him, but he lifted his hands, and the flames vaporized before they touched him.

What the hell? He has magic?

He looked at me one last time and ran out the door.

No!

I ran outside as fast as I could, but he was gone.

"Are you kidding me?" I screamed.

I rushed into the library and searched the floor for the dagger, but it had gone with him.

Shit!

I had him. I had him right here! I eyed my office desk and placed my hands firmly on the top and slid them across, tossing everything onto the floor. I knelt and placed my hands on my head. "I'm going to kill that son of a bitch."

I looked up at the clock on the library wall and it was

three in the morning. I hurried upstairs to check on Melissa, and she was still sound asleep. I grabbed my phone and texted the coven, including Mercy, about what had happened. I didn't care if she was still broken up about everything, she needed to get her shit together and help us with this.

Me: *The killer broke in tonight. It's not Maurice, unless he is using one of his witches. They used magic! Be ready. They have the dagger. I couldn't touch it though. It's laced with some kind of spell. I'll be over to your place in the morning.*

I shut my phone down and laid next to Melissa, watching her breathe in and out, and hoped that our drama would never reach her and damage her like it had so many people we cared about. I couldn't go back to sleep, not while knowing that whoever that was could come back. But if they did, I'd be ready this time to take them out.

CHAPTER TWENTY FOUR

Mercy

Riley and I grabbed a plate of food from Brown's dining hall, and Amber joined us shortly after we sat down, followed by their new pack members, Aaron and Hannah.

"I'm sorry the nightmare is circling back around. How can we help?" Amber asked while I swallowed a bite of my apple.

"Thanks, Amber. I haven't quite figured out that part yet," I admitted, looking over at Aaron and Hannah. They were newly-born werewolves and still had a lot to learn, so when I caught their gaze, they didn't move. They looked at me, ready for instructions, but I didn't run their pack. It wasn't up to me what they decided to do. I didn't need that responsibility, too.

I sighed and wiped my face with a napkin, leaning back into the chair. "Maurice is coming back for revenge. We know he killed the angel who created me. We also know a vampire killed at least three people in East Greenwich and has connections to The Black Horse clan. We feel strongly that it's Maurice, but he's only taking credit for the angel.

The dagger is also missing, which is the only way to kill the coven."

I rubbed my eyes. Just listening to all of that aloud gave me a headache. "Then there's Cami, who was possessed by a demon last year. The demon who created the vampire race. He left a part of his soul inside her, and she's gone. Whatever happened last year destroyed what was left of her. She escaped from Raven's yesterday morning, and now I have to track her down and kill her before she hurts someone. I have to set her free."

I waited as all eyes were on me, and Hannah's jaw dropped. Yeah, maybe they didn't realize what they were getting themselves into when they asked Amber to turn them.

"Look, all of this is the coven's problem, not yours," I told them. "But if you join us, we will forever be in your debt. Truthfully, we always will be on your side, no matter what you choose."

Amber looked down and bit her bottom lip as if she were thinking. "Mercy, a year ago when Riley helped me sniff out my pack, I was devastated to have found them the way we did. Their scent still lingered in those woods from what Kylan had done to them," she explained. "Kylan being dead didn't change anything. Witches and werewolves have been bound together for the same purpose. To kill vampires."

She was right. We weren't divided as witches and werewolves. We were on the same side in the same fight.

Kylan had a plan for months before he tracked me down

to take me out. He punished her pack for protecting me. Thankfully, when he did it, she was looking for me and wasn't caught in the crossfire. She looked for them for months, but little did she know, they had been turned to ash in Salem Woods. With the help of her new pack, they tracked their scent and also Kylan's. They also picked up a human scent, who we assumed he had possessed at the time, to carry out the murders because of the curse Tatyana put on him.

"We will help you take down what is left of Kylan and rid him of this earth for the last time. Just tell us what we need to do. We do this together," Amber said.

Riley smiled at her with pride.

It had taken me a while to accept Riley as a wolf. I didn't want this life for him, not like it was ever my choice to begin with, but seeing how much he had grown and who he had become made me proud. He was happy this way, so it made me happy.

Riley turned to Aaron and Hannah. "Are the two of you ready for this? It's not just Kylan's spirit we're taking out, it's Maurice, too, and whoever is doing the killing, that is, if it's not the same person."

Aaron smiled and spoke for the first time. "We're ready." He grabbed his sister's hand and squeezed. "Whatever you tell us to do, we'll do it."

I pulled my phone out of my purse, and once it powered on, I opened my texts, and there was a group message from Caleb to the coven.

Oh, no.

"I have to head back. I'll call you later, Riley."

"Everything okay?"

"No. The killer broke into Abigail's home last night and attacked Caleb. He's okay, but he mentioned the attacker had the dagger."

"Maurice?" Hannah jumped in, taking interest in her new role in all this.

"They used magic," I explained.

Riley's mouth dropped. "So did Kylan."

I shook my head. "But he's in Cami's body. The person who attacked Caleb was a man. Yes, he could have left Cami's body to possess another, but why would he? From what I witnessed at Raven's, Cami's body is just as strong to do his bidding."

Riley stood and brought me in for a hug. "We're with you until the end."

CHAPTER TWENTY FIVE

Mercy

When I arrived at my house, I saw Caleb's car in the driveway. I shouldn't have turned off my phone. The coven stood around the kitchen table, including Roland.

"Sorry. I had my phone off," I explained, feeling uncomfortable as everyone watched me. I had walked in on something, and I didn't like the way they all looked at me. "I told you, I'm sorry."

Caleb stood and walked over to me. "Mercy, we got another note."

"Another note? When did you get a *first* note?"

He ignored my question and handed me two envelopes. I opened the first one that read, "I have the dagger." I opened the second one, but there was a photo in the envelope instead of a note. I glanced at the picture, trying to understand who I was looking at.

"No!" I cried. "No!"

I closed my eyes, choking back my sob.

It was Sarah.

"I'm so sorry," Leah said, holding my hand and squeezing. "Whoever did this is going to pay. I promise you."

I turned the photo around, no longer able to look at her dead body at the bottom of a shallow grave. There was a note on the back, so I read it out loud.

Now I'll Always Know Your True Face

My stomach lurched as the meaning sunk into my mind. Whoever is doing this knows who Sarah was, knows her power, and knows she was helping me.

"Mercy?" Caleb said, pulling my attention away from the envelope in my hand with a picture of my dead friend. "Now may be the time to consider that it's not Maurice."

"What are you talking about? Of course it's Maurice. He knew her. He was upset that she helped me. It's just like his revenge on Tatyana. He's going after everyone who did him wrong a year ago."

"But it was a witch who attacked him last night. Did you not get the text?" Ezra asked, seemingly annoyed with my rant.

Yes, I got the text, but none of this made sense. "Then he sent a witch to do it. He's always had witches working with him."

"We . . . have another theory," Simon spoke, barely finishing the sentence. I wasn't going to like this theory, and he knew it.

I looked up at Roland. He crossed his arms over his chest, not speaking to me.

"Gee, you're pretty quiet over there, Roland. I'd like to hear this theory, coming from you," I threatened. I knew exactly what they were thinking, and it was bullshit.

"Okay, fine. I believe it's your father," Roland accused while walking toward me. He placed his hands on the table, leaning forward. "You gave him your blood, and now he's using his magic against us."

I shook my head. "No. He wouldn't do that."

"Yes, actually, he would," Roland snapped. "He knew killing those people would draw you out, and he manipulated you into turning him back to the powerful witch he's wanted to be again all these centuries. Now he's taking out the coven because he can't stand that you are more powerful than him."

I slammed my hands on the table and stood to my feet, facing him. "How is that any different than what *you* did to me?"

Roland's face went still. He knew I was right, and he was a complete hypocrite for it.

"I'm not killing people, Mercy," he said.

I shook my head. "And neither is he."

Leah sat next to me and placed her hand on mine, probably hoping her touch would calm me down. "Look, Mercy. We don't want it to be him, but think about it. The killings happened when he was a vampire. Then you turned him, and no one is dying anymore from a bite. Now it's suddenly a witch trying to kill the coven. Your father knows where Caleb lives, so of course he's going to look in our homes first for the dagger. If he has magic, then he could have easily located it."

I thought about everything she had told me, and I still couldn't believe it. I had memories of my father. He loved me. He loved us. He used our elements, so why would he sacrifice us off this earth? True, witches had always been able to harness our powers, but nothing like they had seen since we had been on this earth. It was the difference between chewing one's favorite dish versus swallowing it. They were able to use it and satisfy their senses, but not nourish it.

"You told me that if your father was guilty, you'd kill him yourself," Caleb said. "Has that changed?"

Not that I believed it was my father, but yes, I would kill him if he was trying to hurt us. Of course I would, but I wasn't ready to admit it. Not right now.

"I need to call Joel so we can locate Sarah's body with a spell and bury her," I said, desperately wanting to cry, but I couldn't anymore. The tears wouldn't come.

Everyone remained silent as I turned toward the door and left the house.

CHAPTER TWENTY SIX

Mercy

I t took Joel and me about twenty minutes to find Sarah using a locator spell. She was still there, just like we had seen in the photo. She looked so peaceful, and there weren't any noticeable laceration marks. He must have broken her neck.

We buried her in the East Greenwich Cemetery. I had no one to call about her death. Her parents died years ago, and she didn't have anyone else out here but us. Before she had been taken to Maurice's lair, she'd escaped an abusive relationship back in California. She came to Salem to hide from him, but what she found was a worse nightmare of captivity.

Her friends back home didn't believe her. She had no one she could trust. That's probably why, when Troy showed her kindness in the lair, regardless of the fact that he had pretty much owned her, she welcomed and wanted it.

I spent the rest of the day over at Joel and Derek's home. Derek was still in New York, and after Sarah died, Joel texted Derek and told him not to come back until we found the person responsible.

Was the killer Maurice, my father, or someone else?

Lily and Bradley were still on cloud nine about their engagement, and I didn't want to ruin their excitement by laying out all the crap that had been going on.

Bradley casually mentioned buying a place in Virginia once they got married so they could get away from the area, as he felt it was too dangerous for them. He worked IT from home, so he really could live anywhere, but with everything going on here, he was afraid for her. I tried to explain that it didn't matter where they lived, bad things happened anywhere, and no, I didn't want her to leave me, but it was her life, and maybe she would be safer somewhere else.

Lily also told him about her powers. It was bold, but she'd been wanting to tell him for a long time. He promised to keep her secret, and she left out the part about vampires and werewolves.

One supernatural creature at a time.

We trained over the weekend while planning our next move, which focused on Maurice or my father. I wasn't happy about them accusing him, but if we spied on him, I could prove to the coven that he wasn't involved.

Riley and Amber trained their new pack members, and Dorian and Noah still kept an eye on Maurice.

I texted my father a few times. I kept it brief and didn't give him any indication that there were a few members of my coven thinking he was a murderer. He kept telling me how busy he was, building up his new business, since he wasn't bringing in money from the club anymore and the "other businesses" he conducted while a vampire. He never asked to see me and never asked me if I was okay.

I now felt as if he was, indeed, hiding something. Though, not necessarily that he was the killer.

The other unsettling thing was that it had been two weeks now, and no one from the coven had been attacked, and no dead bodies had come up, that we knew of, anyway.

Yes, under normal circumstances, this would be a good thing, but it also created an unsettling feeling in the pit of my stomach. Every noise in or out of my house ignited my powers. It was as if I was always on. Always ready to strike.

It was eight at night, and Joel had just finished clearing the dinner table. We stuffed ourselves with tacos and coconut milk ice cream.

"Go see Dorian. I have watched the two of you text every night for the last few days. I know you want to see him," Joel said, pushing my phone toward me.

I shook my head. "I want to, but I don't want to give him the wrong idea."

Joel sighed and rolled his eyes. "You're being ridiculous. You know that, right?"

I looked at my phone. I *was* being ridiculous. I decided that if he wanted to see me, then, okay, I would go. If not, I was having another taco and watching a show on Netflix.

I texted him, and his reply came back a few minutes later.

Dorian: *We're home. I'd love to see you.*

"Teleport?" Joel asked, once he saw me place my phone down with a grin on my face.

"Dork, I have a car."

I grabbed my keys and headed out the door.

CHAPTER TWENTY SEVEN

Mercy

Dorian and Noah were in the kitchen when I arrived. He had texted, telling me to just walk in, so I helped myself inside their house.

"Aloha, my beautiful friend," Noah said, kissing me on both cheeks.

"Hey, Noah." I looked at what they were doing and laughed. "You're playing Candyland?"

Dorian's mouth curved at the corner of his lips. "We've never played."

"It's a game for an eight-year-old, Dorian."

They both laughed. "We can always play it with booze," Noah suggested, and I joined in on the laughter. I needed this. I needed this so badly.

After playing Candyland for over an hour, while sober, and Dorian and I catching up on everything we've been doing this last year, I realized I hadn't relaxed like this in months. In fact, I hadn't had this much fun since before my mom attacked me over a year ago. Everything had been constant drama, and I had forgotten how to have fun.

We cleaned up the game pieces, and I entered the kitchen to refill my water. When I turned around, Dorian was standing behind me, and I jumped slightly as it startled me.

"Sorry," he said. He lifted his hand to my cheek, but I didn't flinch or pull away. I let his cold fingers linger on my cheeks, caressing my skin and trailing down to my neck. A chill from the coldness of his hands and the seductive touch caused a strong awareness of my heartbeat, and the hairs prickled on the backs of my arms.

I quickly eyed the clock, pulling my gaze away from him. It read ten in the evening, and if I stayed too late, Joel would ask questions. I really didn't want that. "I have to go," I told Dorian. Noah was already asleep and snoring loudly on the couch.

"I don't want you to go," he confessed, and butterflies hit my stomach again. He was so incredibly sexy, and though my romantic feelings were gone, I wanted him right now.

I was also nervous. I had never been with anyone before. At least, not in this life.

A kiss. Maybe just a kiss.

No, stop, Mercy. You aren't thinking straight.

I looked back at Dorian, and his grin made me weak in the knees. If I didn't leave, we were going to do something I would most likely regret in the morning.

He inched closer to me, and without thinking, I stepped

in his direction, closing the gap between us. I gulped. "Dorian—"

His lips touched mine. The kiss was passionate, intimate, but also seductive.

I won't be able to stop. I can't.

I grabbed the back of his neck and pulled deeper into our kiss. Our tongues swirled around each other, and my body deceived me. I wanted him. I wanted him so badly.

He lifted me up, and I wrapped my legs around his waist. He carried me to the bedroom and closed the door behind us. "Wait!" I gasped. "I've never . . . Dorian, I haven't been with anyone like this."

His eyes widened. "You and Riley?"

I shook my head and he paused, closing his mouth in a straight line but not pulling away. He brushed the side of my hair and tucked it behind my ears.

"I don't know if I'm ready, especially since this is a completely different life from before. I know we were intimate in my past life, but this body, this version of me, is afraid that if we go there . . . Dorian, I'm not sure about my feelings. I don't want to hurt you."

He turned from me, wearing a side smirk, and pulled his shirt off. Then, he walked over to his dresser and pulled out a pair of grey sweatpants. "How about we snuggle?"

I giggled and felt my cheeks flush. "That sounds nice."

My eyes wouldn't leave his body. Seeing him without his shirt on took my breath away. His gorgeous, perfect physique was the first to catch my attention. He handed me a long shirt to wear, and in his other hand were the sweatpants for him. The look he gave me melted my heart and crushed it at the same time. He cared so much for me that he wouldn't push for us to do something I wasn't ready for.

I put on the shirt he handed me and crawled into bed with him. He wore only his boxers and grey sweatpants, and he inched closer to my back and wrapped his arms around me, spooning me closer to him. I shivered at first because his body felt ice cold, but the more we laid there, the warmer our touch became.

"Can you even fall asleep, being that you're a vampire?"

He squeezed me tightly against his chest. "We don't need sleep, but if we choose to fall asleep, we can. I want to sleep next to you tonight."

My cheeks flushed again. "Goodnight."

"Goodnight, Mercy," he whispered into my neck, nuzzling his mouth in my hair and kissing the top of my head.

CHAPTER TWENTY EIGHT

Mercy

I slipped my clothes back on and crept down the stairs, hoping I didn't wake Dorian or even Noah, who had crashed on the couch before we had gone upstairs.

It was two in the morning, and I honestly didn't think I'd fall asleep. I was going to let him hold me, which was nice, but I had to get out of there before morning. I didn't want to talk about the kiss. I wasn't ready to face what all this meant.

"Don't hurt him," Noah said from behind me as I neared the front door. I crunched my face and turned around to face him.

"That's what I'm good at, Noah. Haven't you heard?"

"Not funny, Mercy. He loves you."

I rubbed my eyes and walked up to him, realizing I couldn't walk out the door. Not with Noah. "Okay. But we didn't sleep together. We just . . . cuddled."

"Cuddled?" His eyebrows arched. "That *can* be just as intimate."

I rolled my eyes. "It didn't mean anything."

He huffed. "That's the problem, though, isn't it?"

I didn't respond to that.

"Do you love him again?" he asked.

"No," I admitted too quickly. "I mean, I love him in a different way. It's strange. There is a part of me that feels for Dorian and Caleb. I care about them both, and I would be devastated if something bad happened to them, but I'm not *in* love with them."

"Did the two of you kiss last night?"

I plopped down on the couch in the living room and set my purse next to me. "A couple times, yes," I admitted.

He held up his hand. "That's all I needed to hear."

"What is that supposed to mean?" I asked.

He chuckled. "Did that ridiculous spell you cast prevent you from falling in love again, or did it just take away what you used to have?"

His question caught me off guard. I had to think about it for a minute. I didn't know. Did it mean that I could fall *back* in love with them?

I shrugged.

He leaned back against the couch and grinned. "Don't overthink it."

I wasn't overthinking anything, and this conversation was going to frustrate me if I didn't get out of this house. I didn't owe Noah an explanation, especially since I wasn't sure what it all meant myself.

I grabbed my purse and left the house without saying goodbye to Dorian or talking any further with Noah about what last night meant or could mean. I was ready to get back to my coven.

I didn't get far before I heard Dorian's voice behind me. "Where are you going?"

I sighed deeply and turned around. "I need to get back to my coven."

He shook his head. "Are you kidding me?"

"Please don't do this right now." I held up my hands. "Please, Dorian."

He stopped. He didn't look mad, just hurt. "All right." He relaxed his shoulders and nodded toward his car. "How about I drive you home?"

"I have my car here, Dorian. That's ridiculous."

"I don't want you to leave like this. It's late, and I just want to make sure you get back to your coven safely."

Those words hit me like a ton of bricks. I was hurting him. What the hell was wrong with me? He didn't deserve this. He deserved so much better than this.

So much better than *me*.

"Fine, but what about my car?"

"I'll send Noah to return it in the morning, then he can just fly back as an eagle or something,"

I burst into laughter, and he joined me. He wasn't trying to be funny, but just thinking about Noah getting naked to drive my car so he could transform into a bird and fly back home was comical.

We jumped in Dorian's car, and after a few minutes on the road with neither of us speaking, I broke the silence that hung between us. "Okay. I feel something. I don't know what, but I feel something. I think that, though I don't have romantic feelings like I used to, I *am* attracted to you. Can we start there?"

A huge grin pulled at his lips, then they immediately faded to a straight line. "Mercy, look."

I looked straight ahead and saw someone laying in the middle of the road. "Dorian, stop the car."

Dorian slowed down to a stop just in time to see a redheaded woman lying flat on her stomach. Dorian grabbed my arm when I tried to exit. "Don't get out."

He locked the doors as a fist broke the window next to me. Someone grabbed me firmly by the arm and yanked me out. I tried to plant my feet on the ground and use my powers, but the stranger grabbed my head and pressed against my temples. I couldn't see who it was. It was dark, there were no street lights, and their hold kept my head steady. I heard Dorian's voice scream for me in the distance, but all I could focus on was the pain. The pain was so severe that I couldn't move or think straight.

Then I saw . . . darkness.

"Oh, thank God. You're awake," I heard a man say before he knelt next to the couch where I lay motionless. I flinched.

He had a handsome, kind face, but I didn't recognize him. His skin was smooth, pale, and his eyes were hazel. He grabbed my hand and kissed it gently. "I thought I had lost you."

I yanked my hand back and looked at him with one eyebrow raised. "What happened? Who are you?"

His brows furrowed. "You don't remember? We were attacked tonight."

I didn't remember anything. I was confused about where I was, but most importantly, who I was. I looked down at my hands, examining my skin, then at my shirt. I knew what things were, but not how or why they were.

"Do you know who you are?" he asked me.

I shook my head.

"Your name is Mercy, and we were attacked an hour ago in the middle of the road. It was an ambush. I tried everything I could, but I couldn't get to you.

"We saw someone lying in the street, and the next instant, someone's fist broke the window of my car and pulled you out. Another person grabbed me, and it was like I had no control over my actions. I couldn't save you. They were holding your head firmly, and when another car came around the corner, they let you go and took off. Whatever they did caused you to pass out."

"What did they do to me?"

"From the looks of it, they took your memories," he explained.

My head pounded. "How could someone do that?"

"They must have been a witch."

"A witch?"

The moment that word left my lips, short clips of what I assumed were my life passed through my mind. I saw myself using my hands to levitate leaves that surrounded me as I stood in the middle of a grove of trees.

I felt this man's hand on my arm, and his touch pulled me out of my vision.

His eyes went wide. "You really don't know who you are?" the beautiful man asked.

I looked at him, trying hard to remember more of what I had just seen in that vision, but I still didn't know who *he* was. "Who are you?"

He hesitantly grabbed my hand and smiled. "I'm your boyfriend," he said. "My name is Maurice."

CHAPTER TWENTY NINE

Mercy

I blinked rapidly. "Boyfriend?" I searched my thoughts and tried to remember him. I tried to remember anything. I knew what a boyfriend was, and the concept of a relationship, but people, feelings, and memories were gone. I had a vague flash of being in my home with my mom, who I thought had brown hair. Or was her hair ashy blonde?

I looked around the room. "What is this place?"

He smiled. "It's our home. Does anything here look familiar?"

I looked around the room again, then back at Maurice. The home didn't trigger any memories, but when I looked back at him, I saw a flash of the two of us holding each other on the beach at night, looking out at the ocean. His eyes alone were now familiar.

"I remember something," I said. A smile reached my face. "We were on a beach together at night. I felt your arms around me and the heat of your breath on my neck."

He smiled back. "This is good. This means whatever they did to you, you're strong enough to fight it. Come here." He grabbed my hand to pull me up, but my body tensed the moment he touched my skin. His touch was ice cold. I wasn't sure if it was the coolness that made my body freeze or the fact that this was new and scary to me.

"It's okay. We love each other. I'm not going to hurt you." He leaned into my space and planted his lips on mine. I froze again but let him kiss me.

More memories came to me of the two of us meeting through a familiar face at a bar. I saw the two of us laughing and holding each other close. I felt safe with him in those memories. He cared for me.

He removed his lips from mine. His touch was soft and gentle. It felt nice. A little cold, but nice. He smiled and squeezed my hand. "I'll go get you some water."

I smiled back, but as soon as he walked away, I scanned the room again to see if anything in the home would trigger a memory. I eyed the bookshelf in the corner of the room and looked at the picture frames lining the shelf. I was in them, and so was he. We looked happy together. It was so bizarre to see myself in memories I couldn't remember.

"That was our trip to Italy last summer," Maurice explained. His voice echoed behind me and he joined me at the bookshelf. He handed me the glass of water, and I thanked him. "You had never been outside the country, but you always dreamed of visiting Venice."

He placed his hand on my left hip, pulling me slowly toward him. "We can go there again, just you and me." He tightened his grip, leaning toward my cheek and kissing it softly, gliding his lips across my skin. Goosebumps covered my body, and as amazing as it felt, I pulled away.

"I'm sorry, I just . . ."

"No, I'm the one that's sorry. You don't completely remember me, so you must be freaked out right now. We can take it slowly. I'm sure the memories will come back."

And with that, one did.

I looked back at one of the pictures. "A stranger took this right outside of a shop where you bought me a mask." I paused as the memory became clearer. "The shop was called Ca' Macana."

The name slipped off my tongue. Hopefulness bloomed inside me, and I could hardly contain my happiness. The more I remembered, the more I felt comfortable in this home and near Maurice.

My excitement brought a smile to Maurice's lips. I wished so badly I could remember everything.

I looked around the room again and saw a pentagram plaque against the wall by the console table near a hallway. "I saw a vision when you first talked about what had happened to me," I said. "I saw myself use magic. I can feel it radiate inside me, but I don't know how to use it?" I lifted my hands, examining my fingertips. "I'm not afraid, just confused. Things are starting to make sense, but it's still like a puzzle with missing pieces."

He walked up to me and grabbed my hand. "I can help you. You just have to focus on this green energy you can ignite from your hands. Focus on it reaching your fingertips," he said. I looked down and did as he instructed. I thought about this green energy reaching my fingers, but nothing happened. "I'm sorry. I don't know what I'm doing."

"Focus, Mercy!" This time, his voice was harsh and authoritative. It scared me. "I'm sorry," he said in a softer tone as he grabbed my hand. "I'm overwhelming you. We can try this another day."

I frowned. "You look upset with me."

He took my fingers in his, intertwining them, and brought me closer to him. "I'm not."

He held me in place as he pressed his hands to my cheek, caressing my skin from my cheek bone down to my lips. Then, he let his finger slide down beneath my chin and lifted it. His lips touched mine again. The kiss was deeper this time, more sensual. My body ached for this kiss as if he were someone I had cared for, for years.

I took a deep breath after he let go, and for the first time, I noticed boxes down the hallway. "What's in the boxes?" I asked.

"Oh, I didn't want to bring it up yet, since you're still confused about a lot of things, but, we're moving," he explained.

Moving? I didn't even know where I was yet.

"Where are we now?"

"Salem, Massachusetts. We sold our home, and we're moving to California. I have business there and we have a home waiting for us right on the beach. We leave tomorrow."

I was familiar with the geographical landmarks, but I

had no emotional ties to Salem. I looked out the windows but all I saw was the night sky.

"Shouldn't I be in a hospital?"

"No, Mercy. You don't have amnesia. A witch took your memories away. No doctor can help you."

I thought about what he said. "But why would someone do that to me?"

"Because you're a powerful witch. You were born years ago; 1674 to be exact."

1674?

I've had centuries of memories and I couldn't remember them?

"You, too?" I asked.

"I'm much older," he explained.

"Are you also a witch?"

He smiled. "No. I'm something else." He opened his mouth and his incisors protruded. I gasped and took a step back. My heart pounded hard against my chest. I didn't want to fear this man whom I felt was an important part of my life, but I did.

"You're a . . ."

"Yes, but I won't hurt you. I've never hurt you. I've never hurt anyone. I only drink donor blood from a hospital."

He retracted his fangs, and I relaxed a little, but the fear I had felt at seeing him transform into a vampire still lingered.

I took one more step back to create more distance between us, but he grabbed my hand and gestured toward the hallway. "I'll show you around. Maybe the more you see, the more memories will come back."

During the entire tour of the house, my nerves wouldn't settle. Yes, I had memories with him that felt familiar and safe, but the moment he shared with me that he was a vampire, my defenses stayed up. I couldn't relax. I must have not cared, or why would I be dating him? I had hoped the memories of a world filled with dark creatures only seen in movies would flood over my mind, but they didn't.

I steadied my breathing as we walked down the hall, taking in my surroundings.

We entered a room on the first floor, and it had mostly been packed, but there were a few pieces of furniture, and nothing looked familiar to me. I spotted a dresser in the corner and opened the drawer. Female clothes. Underwear and socks in the first drawer, pajamas in the second, and shorts in the bottom.

"Mine?" I asked.

"I don't live with anyone else. Of course they're yours."

My cheeks flushed with embarrassment, and I looked down again at my apparel, then eyed the bathroom connected to the room. "Mind if I take a shower? I feel dirty. I'd like to clean up and change my clothes."

The truth was, I needed to step away from him so I could absorb everything he had shared with me and the visions that I did have.

"Can I join you?"

I shook my head.

"Okay, I understand. Shower. Take your time," he said before leaving me alone in the room.

I grabbed clean underwear, plaid shorts, and a t-shirt from the nightwear drawer and entered the bathroom.

During my shower, I thought about what I had seen. I knew I was a witch. I felt it, and I saw it in my visions. I didn't fear it, though. The thought hit me that witches are real, so vampires and whatever else was out there should be just as familiar and normal to me. I shouldn't fear it, right? If he was going to hurt me, he would have done it by now.

After a nice, warm shower, I put my pajamas on, pulled my hair into a wet bun, and rubbed some lotion I found in one of the drawers on my face. I brushed my teeth and re-entered the bedroom. Maurice lay on the bed, resting on the pillow closest to the window. He had the blankets pulled back, leaving an empty space below the other pillow.

Was I supposed to lay with him? Of course he'd assume that, if that was our normal routine.

I didn't want to upset him, so I climbed into bed and laid down. "Maurice, I don't . . . I'm not ready to do anything with you."

He smiled. "I won't touch you, yet. But we've been together for over three years, Mercy. I hope all your memories come back so we can get back to where we were before we were attacked."

I gathered my thoughts, then asked, "Are we really moving? Shouldn't we be trying to find out who took my memories away, and more importantly, why?"

He shook his head. "This isn't new. You have been targeted for centuries. You are a powerful witch, and those who want to hurt you will stop at nothing. That's why we have to leave this place. We need to find a new home where your enemies can't find you."

I looked up at the ceiling, still feeling confused and unsure about everything, but the fact that he was the only one here, the only one I had even the slightest memories with, happy memories, showed me I could maybe trust him. I had to. I had nowhere else to go.

"Okay," I said, smiling and placing my hand on his cheek. "I'm sorry I don't remember everything, but I promise I'll keep trying."

He leaned in and kissed me on the forehead, then the cheek, then the lips. His hands lingering by my hips, caressing my skin, and inching under my shirt and up my stomach. I placed my hand on his, stopping him. It felt good. My God, did it feel good, but I couldn't be intimate with someone I didn't remember, let alone a vampire who frightened me.

He pulled his hand out and kissed me on the lips. "Goodnight, Mercy."

I closed my eyes, facing away from him now, but his arms were wrapped around me, holding me close to his chest. He didn't try to kiss or touch me, but he held me until we fell asleep.

CHAPTER THIRTY

Mercy

The next morning, I awoke to the stench of bacon. I had to hold back the nausea as I entered the kitchen.

"Good morning, beautiful. Here." He placed three strips of bacon on a plate, and I just looked at it. "Are you not hungry? I'm sorry, I don't eat food. I only drink blood. Was there something else you wanted me to make you?"

I looked up at him and back down at the bacon. "Not this." I admitted. "I don't think I ate things like this."

"Bacon?" He paused. "Oh, meat? No, you definitely eat meat."

"Are you sure? Because the smell alone is making me nauseous."

His face grew hard. I must have offended him. He picked up the plate of bacon and let the strips slide off the plate and into the trash. "I can make you something else," he said, "like a smoothie?"

When I smiled and nodded, his frown faded into a grin and he perked up. The change in his mood helped me relax.

He pulled frozen strawberries from the freezer, grabbed

orange juice from the fridge, and poured them all into a blender.

"Bon appetite," he said as he handed me my smoothie.

"Thank you." I smiled and sipped slowly. It was good. The strawberry and orange juice was the perfect combo I had been craving.

"I have a few friends stopping by here this morning, then a moving company is coming over to help us pack the rest of our things."

"What are we taking? That's quite a trip to take all this stuff."

"Most is being sold or being donated. We'll ship a few things to Huntington Beach. We just need to pack our clothes and some of the personal items we own."

Maurice's phone rang and he answered on the second ring.

Once he answered, he excused himself from the kitchen.

After I finished my smoothie, I stepped outside and took a deep breath, taking in the air around me. I looked over the balcony and saw a few deer run through the clearing near us.

Where were we exactly? All I saw was a forest surrounding us. No other houses, not even a road.

I turned around and Maurice stood near the sliding door, watching me, but he didn't step outside. I walked up to him and slid the door back open. "It's nice today. Maybe we can have breakfast out here."

He shook his head. "I can't."

"You can't come outside?"

I looked up. Rays from the morning sunrise shone onto the deck. "Oh, of course. I'm sorry. Vampires can't go in the sun, right?"

He nodded.

But then I thought about where we were moving today. "But aren't we moving to California? It's sunny 300 times a year there. Seems a vampire would avoid a place like that."

He looked irritated, keeping his mouth in a straight line and flaring his nostrils when I asked my question, but I couldn't understand why. Was he just going to hide inside all day?

He relaxed his expression and grinned. "That is why we are moving there. There's a witch in Los Angeles who's a good friend of mine. She plans to create a more permanent solution for vampires. We lost all hope when we realized we were wrong about the witch who we'd thought for centuries was going to be the key to remove the curse of the sun. So, now, we have to figure it out on our own."

As much as I still feared being this close to a real vampire, the fact that he couldn't enjoy the sun beaming down on him every day made me feel sorry for him.

"I have a meeting with a few of my colleagues. How about you read a book or watch something on my computer in the office? I have a bookshelf full of books you love. Maybe they'll trigger more memories."

I looked past him and saw a man and woman standing in the family room. I didn't recognize them, no memories came back, but they were pale, just like Maurice. A vampire trait, I assumed. An anxious feeling came over me as I narrowed my eyes at them. Maurice being a vampire is one thing. He was someone I remember caring for. Those two in the family room were strangers. Undead strangers. My stomach twisted in knots, and I wanted to hide in my room until they left.

"Please, come meet my friends first."

I stared at him with a pleading look, but he smiled and grabbed my hand gently. "It's okay. They won't hurt you."

He escorted me to the front room where the two stood and gestured to the dark-haired guy with light scruff on his face. "This is Julian. He joined my business a few months ago. And this is Jade." I looked to the redhead next to Julian. She had dark auburn hair and her skin was a bright shade of white. She almost looked like she had no pigmentation at all aside from her red hair.

They both smiled at me awkwardly, and it made me uncomfortable. Their eyes spoke to me as if they knew something I didn't, and they seemed to take pleasure in that.

"Jade and I have known each other for years. She has been traveling around Europe this last year and joined my company a month ago," Maurice explained.

I swallowed hard and felt a painful lump in my throat go down slowly. Something was off about all three of them.

Way off.

"What do you do, Maurice? For work?" I asked.

He smiled as if he was excited that I was finally asking the important questions. "I run a blood donation corporation," he said, and I looked at him with skepticism. "You see, not every vampire wants to drink from humans," he said. "So, we provide a solution by draining blood from willing donors. Then, we sell it for profit."

"They're all willing?" I asked. Just the mere thought of blood made me queasy.

He chuckled, and Julian and Jade joined in. "Most of them, sweetheart. You see, that same witch who we thought could save us now wants to kill us off. We've also learned of witches who can manipulate someone's face. If a vampire doesn't realize they're drinking from her under this disguise, they would become human again. We can't have that."

I swallowed deeply. "Well, I don't know. I'd think being a human would be a good thing, unless you like being this way."

After I said this, all three narrowed their eyes at me and tightened their lips.

I gulped but continued, hoping my voice didn't sound too nervous. "How do you know the donors aren't this witch? In disguise?"

He reached up and brushed the hair from my cheek, then leaned in and kissed it gently. "We inject them with a potion. If she changes back, then we know. If they don't, we take as much as they're willing to give, *without* killing them."

"That . . . that sounds wrong, Maurice."

He walked closer to me, and I backed up. "Which part, my love?"

I looked at the others, then back to Maurice. "All of it."

His frown turned into a side smirk. "What is the difference between a human donating their blood to save another human's life and what we're doing?"

I didn't know how to answer this without upsetting him. He had been nice since I awoke on that couch yesterday, but I really didn't know him.

He shrugged when I didn't answer. "It doesn't matter. Once we move, I won't be running that business anymore."

I looked at Jade, who was snickering to herself.

"Why not?" I asked.

"Because that witch is no longer a problem," he explained, and that was the last thing he needed to say. I was a witch, which meant this other witch he spoke of could be a friend. She could be family.

"I'm going to go use the restroom. Excuse me." I shifted toward the hallway, but Maurice grabbed my arm and I winced. "You're hurting me. Please let go."

"Is there something else you'd like to say to me?" he asked.

"Nope." I shook my head. "I just really have to pee."

He flashed me a forced smile that made my stomach churn. It was sadistic and unkind. "Be quick. Jade and Julian are taking us to the airport. We leave in an hour."

He released my arm, and I hurried to the bathroom. I didn't need to go. I just needed a moment away from those three. I looked in the mirror. I didn't recognize myself, and I desperately needed to know if everything he'd told me since I awoke on his couch was true. Why would anyone try to hurt me? That question didn't seem to press Maurice. He should be wondering why this happened and trying to find a solution, not moving across the country. I couldn't just leave on a plane with someone who was a stranger to me, regardless of these fragments of memories I had of him. I had to get out of here.

After I looked around the bathroom for anything to defend myself with if he or his two minions tried to stop me, I saw the window above the bathroom sink. I double checked that I had locked the door and moved to the window, unlocked it, and slowly cranked it open. I pulled myself up, climbed out the window, and dropped to the grassy lawn below me. Since it was daylight out, I was able to check around at my surroundings to locate an escape, except, there wasn't one. The only relief I felt was that the three vampires were still inside, and even if they wanted to come outside, the sun would stop them.

I snuck around the corner just in case, and when I turned, I ran into a chest.

His chest.

He looked down and smiled. "Where on earth do you think you're going, my love?" Maurice asked with a sinister grin. I looked behind him, and there stood Jade and Julian. The sun beamed down on them as if my theory was only something you'd see in a movie.

"Magic," he said.

I blinked. "What?"

"You're asking yourself how we are able to walk in the light, aren't you?"

I nodded.

"You see, when we found out that this witch couldn't actually allow us to walk in the light unless she turned us human, we found a witch who created a temporary spell for when we needed it. It only lasts about ten minutes, so we need to get back in the house."

When I tried to back up, he grabbed my arm and yanked me toward him. "I would never be with someone as evil as you," I said.

He gripped my arm so hard I knew there would be a bruise the next day. "I know you wouldn't."

That was when I screamed. I screamed the entire time he dragged me by the hair back into the house, flailing my arms and kicking my legs. I screamed for help, but nobody came. I wailed as I scanned my surroundings. It was just us. The house stood deep into a property, surrounded by nothing but trees. No neighbors, no road, nothing. No one would hear me. Maurice told me that my powers came from my hands, so I lifted my hand and focused on this energy I supposedly possessed, but nothing happened.

Maurice threw me into a corner of the family room, and Julian walked toward me. I cowered the closer he came.

"Let's try this again, shall we?" he said to Julian. "She is to remember she's a witch, but our attacker took her ability to use her magic. She's too powerful of a witch to not feel her powers inside her. She also needs to know about the existence of vampires so she isn't afraid of me," Maurice commanded. "Just make sure she doesn't know *everything* about who she is."

"Her mind is too strong to take away everything, Maurice, but I'll try."

They spoke to each other as if I weren't even in the room. My heart still pounded hard against my chest.

Julian looked down at me as panic filled my entire body. This guy Julian wasn't a vampire. He was a witch.

He fisted my hair and yanked me down to my knees and placed his hands over each side of my temples, then chanted. My head screamed in pain, and fear engulfed every part of me . . . until it went dark.

CHAPTER THIRTY ONE

Caleb

I looked at Dorian's car on the side of the road at the corner of Chestnut and Parker Rd. Someone had broken the front windows, and Mercy's purse was still on the floor of the passenger's side. I turned to Lily and saw Bradley holding her tightly. She cried in his arms. Turning to my right, Riley was barely holding himself together. His hands were in a tight fist, and if it weren't for Amber caressing his arms to calm him, he'd transform into his werewolf form.

I understood this type of fury. Mercy wasn't off sacrificing herself again. Someone kidnapped her, along with Dorian. It must have been an ambush Dorian couldn't stop, because he was a good fighter and he would have fought for her life. He was likely dead, but not her. I could feel her. I also knew who was responsible.

This also meant that we were right about it not being Maurice who took the dagger. If he had it, she'd be dead.

"That's it. I'm calling the cops," Bradley said, throwing his hands up and reaching into his pocket.

"Lily," I said, hoping she'd stop this nonsense before it got out of hand.

She grabbed Bradley's hand to stop him, but when he resisted, she sprawled her fingers out and chanted. Bradley dropped the phone, not able to use his hand.

"Are you kidding me, Lily? You said you'd never use your powers on me!" he screamed. He looked more afraid than upset.

"And you promised you'd keep my secret after I told you." Lily's face softened. "What do you think the cops will do to us once they find out what really is happening here? Huh? What do you think Maurice will do to the cops you plan to call when and if they catch up with him?"

Bradley relaxed his shoulders and Lily released the magic that had kept him from using his hand.

I turned back to Riley. "Go ahead."

Amber, who was still trying to relax him, lifted her hand from his arm and they both crouched down. After they transitioned into their wolf forms and sniffed the ground around the street, they sniffed the car, her purse, the glass on the ground, and turned to each other. Amber and Riley tapped their noses together as if it were some kind of communication between the two.

Riley turned back to his human form and stood in front of me, naked. It was a bit awkward, but he seemed to not care, as if it were completely normal to be standing in the buff. "Okay, we have the scent. I smelled both a vampire and a witch."

"Maurice?" I asked.

He shook his head. "I didn't recognize the scent."

"Dammit," I cursed. I then looked at Lily. "It doesn't mean it's not him. He had people who worked for him before. He most likely has a following now."

We got back into our cars, and I phoned Joel to let him know what we had found out.

Once back at Abigail's, I entered the kitchen and poured myself a glass of whiskey. It had been a while since I drank hard liquor, but I felt numb at this point. The extent of Maurice's fury left him willing to do anything to her to seek revenge. The perfect punishment. If he was willing to kill an angel with a sword, with no remorse, what was he willing to do to Mercy?

I sipped my drink as I paced the floor.

"We'll find her," Roland assured me. He had been standing in the doorway of the kitchen. I stopped dead in my tracks when he stepped in front of me. "Look, this is Mercy we're talking about. You know that she is going to get herself out of this. She's alive. That you know."

He was right. She was alive, but what had he done to her? What was he planning? Was she even here in Rhode Island? Had he taken her somewhere else?

I lowered my head and looked at the whiskey, then back

up at Roland. "I've got to go," I said while handing him my glass. "Here. Knock yourself out."

And with that, I left to find Melissa.

I knocked on the door to her apartment until she opened the door. She was wearing a green, spaghetti-strap nightgown that came down to her knees. Her tattoos showed and her hair was pulled back into a low braid.

"Hey, Caleb."

I took a step in without an invitation and placed my hands on the sides of her neck, staring at her. "Hey, you," I said. "Can I stay here tonight?"

"Did you find her?" She ignored my question.

I shook my head.

"Is that why you're here? You're sad she's gone, and you need me?"

I winced at her question. It stung because she was right. No, not completely. I cared about Melissa. She was sexy, funny, and smart, but I was hurting tonight. I was hurting and I needed her.

"I don't know," I confessed as I released her and walked toward her bedroom. She looked at me, her head tilted to the right. She was probably contemplating what she wanted to do.

She walked toward me and held out her hand. After I took it, I escorted her to the bedroom. She turned to face me once we reached the bed. I leaned down, kissed her gently, and she kissed me back, so I deepened the kiss.

We kissed for a minute, and my hands reached down to her shirt and lifted it above her head. She placed her hands on my chest and smiled, giving me the invitation I needed.

We didn't sleep. We didn't talk about the pain I felt or the shame she'd feel in the morning, knowing I wasn't completely with her. But it didn't matter. We both knew it didn't matter. She was what I needed, and she'd let me have her.

CHAPTER THIRTY TWO

Mercy

California! Maurice was taking me to California. I'd always wanted to visit the Pacific Ocean. I also wasn't just visiting, I was going to live there. According to Maurice, our backyard faced the ocean!

Maurice grabbed my hand as we descended the stairs from his private jet. It was evening, so they didn't need a spell cast on them to get them from point A to point B to avoid the sunlight.

Jade grabbed my suitcase, and Julian waited at the bottom of the stairs next to the limo and opened the door for us as we approached.

It was only a short drive to Huntington Beach. Maurice owned a private runway right outside the city. I was excited to be in our new home. The flight wasn't terrible, but I was ready to sleep.

Maurice was quiet during the drive, but as we pulled into our new driveway, he kissed me on the lips. His kiss was kind and gentle. His mouth tasted like the dark, red wine and chocolate served to us during the flight.

I hadn't had the chance to explore our home yet. The

lights were dim, and Maurice led us to our bedroom. From what I did see, the home was already fully furnished and ready for us.

Maurice turned to me and pulled the blanket up as we lay in bed. He brushed the stray hair from my face and pulled me closer to him. "I love you, Mercy." His voice was gentle, and his words were familiar. I was still trying to recall all the memories I had lost, but the sound of his voice, his words, rang familiar and brought me comfort. I felt safe. "Tomorrow, I have some business to attend to, but I'll have Julian escort you around the city. Does that sound nice?"

I nodded, smiled, and kissed him on the lips. "Thank you. Goodnight, Maurice."

I closed my eyes, no longer able to fight my exhaustion, and let my dreams take me away.

Did I always dream like this? I couldn't remember. I guessed most people don't really remember their dreams, but everything around me felt familiar, like I had entered this world in my subconsciousness. Maybe my dreams would help me remember everything.

A man with features similar to Maurice's walked up to me, holding a red scarf in his hand. He lifted it above my head and wrapped my hair in it. "Tradition," he said.

I looked over and Maurice stood on a stage. The wind from the open windows around us blew his hair around in a beautiful dance.

I blinked once and was standing outside. A black wolf stood by a light grey one who was a little bigger than the other. They slowly crept toward me, but I didn't feel threatened. I didn't fear for my life. They were enchanting.

The grey wolf was so close, I could feel its breath on my arm. It nudged me as I looked over to the other, but I wasn't sure what they were wanting me to do. "What do you want?"

He lifted his snout as the other joined in, howling toward the moon above us. It was dark and a cool breeze blew across my skin. Their howls echoed in my ears. As their voices rang, I looked down to my hands. They were glowing bright green. The light was bright, and the feeling was so powerful, it nearly took my breath away.

I sat bolt upright, gasping for air and clutching the sheet close to my body. I looked over to Maurice.

He looked asleep but I wasn't sure how deep of a sleep a vampire could get. Was he simply resting his eyes or off into a dream?

I crawled out of bed, entered the balcony attached to the master bedroom, and looked out at the water. The waves crashed onto the shore, rolling over each other and then thinning out as the tide pulled up and the current brought it back to the deep sea. The full moon beamed down on the surface of the water, creating a bright glow. The moon was bright tonight, almost as bright as it was in my dream.

I brought my hands up to my body like I had done in my dream. I held my palms in front of me, focusing on the feeling I had felt just moments before I opened my eyes. Then, my fingertip glowed ever so faintly.

The more I focused on them, the more intense the

glowing became. It grew until my hands radiated emerald green. It was so beautiful and powerful. My body felt a lustful hunger I didn't know existed.

How powerful am I?

What does this power even do?

I heard something stir behind me, and I concealed the light. A moment later, Maurice joined me on the balcony, wrapping his arms around my waist. I thought I would be excited about what I had discovered, but I had a sinking feeling in the pit of my stomach. I needed to keep this a secret from him. When I awoke from our attack a few days ago, he had told me that I was a witch, but that the ability to use those powers was taken from me. It was all a lie, unless whatever happened to me was no longer working. I could use them, and it felt incredible.

"What are you doing out here?" he asked me.

I stared at the moon as if I were drawn to it like a moth to a flame. There was a world out there that I didn't fully know or understand. Slowly, memories were coming back to me about my life with Maurice, but that was it. Everything outside that box was still missing. I knew my name and places I had been with Maurice, but what about me? I had no memories of who *I* was. Who was Mercy beyond this relationship? What did I do for a hobby? Was I funny? Serious? Kind?

Why were memories of activities I'd done with Maurice and my feelings for him there but nothing else?

"I couldn't sleep . . . bad dream," I explained.

He hugged me tighter around my waist, pulling my backside into him. "Do you want to talk about it?"

I shook my head. "I'm going to grab some water and go back to bed." I wiggled out of his grasp. "I'll be right back up."

When I turned around, he looked pained, or angry, but I didn't stop to make him feel better. I left him standing on the balcony and headed inside.

Upon entering the kitchen, I grabbed a glass from the cabinet and filled it with filtered water from the fridge.

I looked around the fully furnished family room. Maurice had told me that a local furniture company had set up the house a week ago, so we didn't need to worry about unpacking anything aside from our personal belongings that would show up from the moving truck in a few days.

I hadn't been able to explore the new house yet. We got in late last night and turned in early due to the exhaustion brought on by our travels.

The house was dark, and not just because it was three in the morning or because all the lights were turned off. But dark. The walls had been painted a dark grey, the furniture was all black, and the cherry floors were highly polished. From each window hung black, thick drapes which I assumed were to black out the sun for Maurice's benefit.

I didn't mind the dark colors—they felt warm and inviting—but they created a haunting feeling around me. A strange, dark home I had never been. It wasn't mine, not really. Maurice wasn't my husband. I didn't work. I was a stranger in *his* space, whether he wanted me there or not.

I noticed a door at the end of the hallway. The door was different from the others—dark brown and thick. There were three locks, and there wasn't even the tiniest crack between the bottom of the door and the floor. The handle resembled a car's steering wheel, but it was made of metal.

I took a step toward the door when I heard someone clear their throat behind me. I jumped.

"Maurice doesn't like to keep his money in a bank. The safe is off limits," Jade said in a harsh tone.

"I was just curious," I said, hoping she'd leave me alone. "Besides, it's secured. I'd need a key."

Her face grew hard. She did *not* like me.

"I didn't even realize you were here in the house with us. This place is huge. Did I wake you?" I asked, hoping if I came off like I cared about her feelings, she'd back off.

"Does that bother you?" she asked. Her question didn't sit well with me, but I didn't want to argue with her at three in the morning.

I'll just talk to Maurice about it.

"No. I just didn't expect you here, that's all. You startled me."

She laughed and took a step toward me. "You're not the only one he wants."

I knew what she meant, and it made me sick. I didn't want to be here. Not standing in front of her, not even in this house.

"Jade, what the hell are you doing?" Maurice asked her, his voice filled with fury and disgust.

"Nothing, Master. I was just stopping her from snooping."

He glared at her. He was pissed. "It's not snooping when it's your own damn house," he said through gritted teeth. The moonlight streaming through the windows cast a garish glare on his protruding fangs.

She stopped, her face frozen with fear, and a familiarity to her words struck me like a ton of bricks.

Master.

Where had I heard that?

"Forgive me. I just came to the kitchen to grab some blood. I'll be leaving now."

She was afraid of him. No, not afraid. She was terrified.

CHAPTER THIRTY THREE

Mercy

I didn't ask Maurice about the safe. I didn't ask why Jade had called him Master. I didn't want to know. All of this was unsettling, and my instincts told me that everything they'd been feeding me since I woke up yesterday morning was a lie.

"Can you pour me some more?" I asked Maurice, who was holding the coffee pot.

He walked near me, topped off my coffee, and leaned back against the counter after setting it back down on the warmer.

I sipped my coffee slowly, shifting my gaze up at him. He only stared at me, as if he were waiting for me to speak. But I had nothing to say. I only wanted to see what was inside that safe.

"I'm going to Los Angeles this morning to get my office set up. Julian will be in and out, and if you would like to explore the city, make sure he is with you," he said.

"Not Jade?"

"You'll be out in the daylight too long. The spell Julian creates is only temporary," he explained.

"Oh, yeah."

He came around the corner, leaned down, and kissed my head. I didn't look up. Just the feeling of his lips on my head sent a wave of uncertainty coursing through my mind. After last night, something wasn't right, and I was going to find out what it was.

As he neared the front door, he turned to face me again. "Oh, and Mercy?" I looked at him intently. "Sorry if Jade made you feel uncomfortable last night. This is your home, too."

I nodded in understanding, and as he left me standing in the kitchen, I said, "Wait, did Julian cast that spell so you can walk to the car safely?"

He laughed. "Yes, my love. The limo has tinted windows, and we're parking in an underground parking structure at the office. I only need his help from the house to the car. It will be dark when I leave the office tonight."

"Oh. Okay, well, have a good day, then. I'll see you tonight."

I walked toward the front, stared out the porch windows, and watched him drive away.

Where was Julian? I really needed to get out of this house.

Speaking of the devil, just as I put my plate in the sink, Julian strolled into the kitchen.

"I have to run a few errands in town for Maurice. Would you like to join me and get some sun?"

Thank goodness. I was already suffocating in this place, and this was my new home.

"Let me put on my shoes," I said, as I rushed to get ready.

After ten minutes, I met Julian at the front door. "Okay, let's go." My tone came off a little too excited. I didn't want to let him know I was already hating it here.

We drove only a few blocks until we hit Main Street. There were people everywhere. On the crowded sidewalks were a few street vendors who lined the boardwalk, and couples walked hand in hand on the pier. A few young skate-boarders and even a man playing his guitar for money could be seen on the corner of Pacific Coast Highway and Main. It was quite different than Salem.

Julian parked along the street, and we walked toward the pier. "I need to speak to a colleague and give him a few items. Enjoy the beach."

Really?

I saw a man looking at us on the pier, wearing a polo shirt and khaki pants. He held a cell phone in one hand and a briefcase in the other. As curious as I was about this little exchange of theirs, my eyes shifted to the waves crashing onto the shore. It was stunning at night, but this was something else. I stepped onto the sand and vague memories washed over me. Perhaps I used to live by a beach near Salem.

I walked toward the water, feeling the grainy sand between my toes. I dropped my shoes at the perfect spot and sat down, crossing my legs underneath me. I closed my eyes and a single tear fell.

I didn't understand it. Why was I crying? I kept them shut and took a deep breath in.

"Lily, you're too close to the water," a woman called, and my eyes shot open.

Lily?

A little girl, maybe four years old, ran toward her mother who sat on a beach towel, carrying a bucket of salt water. "Sorry, Mommy," she said. The mother pointed her finger at her daughter, then toward the shore as if teaching her the dangers of getting too close to the water when she wasn't next to her. I couldn't hear what they were saying, but I could see the worry in her mother's eyes.

Lily. It was a beautiful name. A familiar name at that. Maybe I had a friend back home by that name.

I must remember to ask Maurice about it.

Just as I made myself at home on the beach, Julian cleared his throat behind me, "We'll come back. It's nice out here, isn't it?"

"It's beautiful. Have you been to a beach before?"

He laughed. "Yes, Mercy. There are several beaches on the east coast. My coven had a beach house up at Cape Cod at one point, too."

"Did I have a coven?" I asked.

He shook his head. "No."

His answer was so abrupt, and he reached out his hand. I took it.

"Why not?"

He crinkled his nose. "Mercy, I have business to attend. Let's go."

I didn't press the issue. He obviously didn't want to answer me and was upset about me even asking. It was a logical question.

"Ouch, Mommy. It hurts," the same little girl cried, and I stopped to look back at them. Her mother held on to her daughter's foot. There was blood.

Oh, no.

Her mother ruffled through her purse and looked scattered while her little girl screamed and cried, holding her bloodied foot.

I didn't hesitate before rushing toward them.

"Mercy, stop. It's not our business," Julian warned, but I ignored him.

He caught up with me and grabbed my arm, but I yanked it away. "What are you doing? Don't touch me!"

If looks could kill—that was how angry he looked. His eyes blazed and his hands were in fists.

I looked back at the mom and daughter, not caring about Julian, and approached them. "May I?" Tears rolled down the mom's face.

"She stepped on broken glass. There's so much blood, and I can't find my Band-Aids."

"It's okay," I said as I grabbed the girl's foot. I had no idea what I was doing. I didn't have any Band-Aids, either, but I felt like I could help her.

I placed my hand on her foot and focused on the power I had ignited in the middle of the night. It was easier this time. I didn't have to think about it. My powers came through and wrapped around her little foot, and when I removed my hand, the laceration was gone.

Wow. Okay, now I know what that power does.

The little girl stopped crying, and when I looked at the mom, her jaw dropped, and she began to shake.

"It's okay," I said, but she quickly grabbed her daughter. She didn't even thank me. She was scared of me. She stood up to run with her daughter in her arms, but Julian intervened, placing his hands on both their heads, causing her to fall to her knees. They both kicked and struggled with him, but he held to them firmly until they relaxed and went into a trance-like state.

I looked around to see if anyone was watching. Everyone was so preoccupied with their own lives, no one saw what had happened.

"What are you doing to them? Let them go."

He did, but then bent down, grabbed the beach bucket of ocean water, and poured it over the blood on her foot, washing it clean.

When he finished cleaning her foot, they opened their eyes and looked at both of us. "Who are you guys? What are you doing here?"

"Miss, your daughter was screaming. We came to make sure everything was okay."

"We're fine!" she snapped as she pulled her daughter close.

"We'll leave. Sorry to bother you," I said as I got up and walked away, Julian right behind me. He caught up with me and gripped my arm.

"Don't ever use your magic like that in public. I don't care if someone is dying. You don't do it."

I stopped walking. "Shouldn't you be happy I have magic back?"

Julian's jaw tensed. "We'll talk about it back at the house." He stomped off, and this time, I staggered behind.

"So, your power is that you can take memories away?" I asked, then stopped again. My feet wouldn't move anymore as the realization of what the hell just happened hit me.

I backed up and he knew. He knew that I knew.

"It was you," I gasped, backing up another foot. "You did this to me."

I held up my hands when he tried to approach.

He chuckled, holding up his own hands in defeat. "Fine. Yes. I did this to you. You're still coming back to the house with me. I think I'll cut my errands short today."

"I'm not going anywhere."

When I turned to run, he was at my back and fisted my hair, pulling me under the pier so no one could see. He slammed me against the wooden post holding up the dock. I placed my hands on his chest and blasted him across the sand until he hit the water.

Alright. My powers also do that.

What the hell was I doing? I needed to run, but I just stood there.

Run, you idiot!

But I didn't. He was still knocked out, and the water covered his face. He'd drown if I didn't pull him out.

"Dammit," I cursed out loud.

I'll pull him up to the sand then run.

I grabbed his legs and pulled him farther onto the sand. I wasn't going to be responsible for someone's death, even if they were a lying creep.

Once he was safe from drowning, I turned toward the parking lot to run, but I felt his grip on my ankle and he yanked, pulling me down on my stomach. I lifted my hands, but he was already at my temples, chanting.

CHAPTER THIRTY FOUR

Caleb

It had been a week since Mercy disappeared. A week where we could still feel her, but we didn't know where she was. I cursed the spell Joel had cast that made her undetectable.

Melissa squeezed her arms around me, her head lying on my chest. I turned our show off, which we weren't really watching to begin with. Melissa had fallen asleep an hour in, and my mind had drifted to wondering where Mercy could be.

Anger brewed inside me, and I wished to God I'd soon get the opportunity to take Maurice's life.

I rubbed Melissa's arm, kissed her on top of her head, and slowly wiggled out of her grasp. Her head laid gently on the pillow next to us and I pulled the blanket over her before heading toward the liquor cabinet. After I poured myself a glass of whiskey, Simon walked into the kitchen.

As a coven, we had decided to stay together at all times, given the circumstances. At Abigail's mansion, there was plenty of room and a security system in place if anyone were to breach the walls again. I just had to remember to set the alarm.

"How about one for me, too, yeah?" Simon asked. I was happy to oblige. I poured him a glass, and we clinked our glasses together. "Cheers, brother."

"I'm going by Melissa's tomorrow to pick up a few more of her things. I'm not okay with her being alone until we've taken care of the Cami situation and the killer," I explained.

"It's been quiet," he reminded me.

"Not always a good thing." I looked toward the stairs. "Everyone else asleep?"

He nodded. "I just can't shut my mind off. It's crazy that you lay your head down and your dreams appear, and the first thing you see is her face. Like, she's here, but not."

I placed my glass on the counter and folded my arms across my chest. "I know what you mean."

"What time does Roland want us downstairs for the meeting?" he asked.

"Nine."

Simon looked up at the wall clock, and my eyes followed. It was three in the morning, "All right, we need to crash."

He held up the last remaining drips of whiskey, chugged it, and left upstairs before me. I grabbed Melissa from the couch, cradled her in my arms, and carried her to my room.

I tapped my coffee mug impatiently with my index finger as

we waited for Roland to speak. He took a call right as we finally sat down for the meeting, so now, we had to wait even longer. Ezra was the most impatient one in the coven, so he made sure to tap his foot as loudly as he could against the floor so Roland would hurry up the call and get on with it.

"Are you sure he wants me here?" Melissa asked.

"You have helped us out more than most. You're a part of this as long as you want to be."

My words didn't ease her discomfort. I wanted the coven to know that she wasn't going anywhere. We had talked last night about being exclusive. I wasn't going to date anyone else, and we cared about each other, but given the fact that she was sitting in a room with a coven of powerful witches, she wouldn't truly feel welcomed, as much as I tried to make her feel like she was part of our family.

Roland finished his call and stood. "Sorry about that. We have a lot to discuss, so I'll get on with it." He glanced around the table, probably taking note that everyone was accounted for. "When the vampires learned what Mercy's blood would really do, Maurice orchestrated a team to find another solution," he explained.

I huffed, and Ezra joined me. "There isn't another solution. It's impossible."

Roland shook his head. "That we know of."

"What are you saying? That Maurice found a way to do what he *thought* Mercy could do?" Leah asked, looking around the table.

"When he was here, he built a business supplying blood

to vampires for profit. He's gained quite a client list, and according to Alexander, he was working on locating a coven of witches, who aren't the easiest to find, to help him create a potion that, when given to a vampire, would block the UV rays from the sun and prevent them from burning to ash."

My jaw dropped, and when I looked around, everyone else at the table looked just as dumbfounded. "How is it that I've never heard of a spell that has the power to do that? And how do you even know this information?"

"Marcus. He heard Maurice talking about it before Maurice left the clan. Marcus brought it up to me a few months ago, but until I had more information, I didn't want the coven involved."

I slammed my hands down on the table, and Melissa jumped beside me. "Are you serious? This could be the very reason he took her."

Roland shook his head at me. "Mercy can protect herself. There are more vampires and witches involved in this than we know. This is the only way to find the witches who have turned to the dark side and take them down. I'm confident Mercy will be able to escape and help lead us to where they're at. We need to know what they're up to. Perhaps she can even take them down from the inside."

I was about to punch my own father in the face. I stood up, balling my hands into fists. "So, you allowed her to be bait?"

"I've always done what was best for the coven. Sit. Down."

Fire ignited in my hands, and I held my palms up.

"Caleb, oh, my God. He's your father. What are you doing?" Melissa cried as she placed her hand on my arm, trying to calm me, but I only brushed her hand away.

"You're a traitor," I threatened. "Twice now, you've put Mercy's life in danger. We can no longer trust you!"

Ezra stood and pulled his hands out, and a light brown glow radiated from his palms. The trees rattled outside the windows surrounding us. "Traitor," he said.

Simon stood, a bit slower than Ezra, and pulled his hands out as a white glow radiated from them. A gust of wind whipped through the windows and into the kitchen.

Leah remained sitting. She looked up at us with fear in her eyes, but she was loyal and would always have the coven's backs, so she, too, stood and looked at Roland. She pulled her hand to her side. A light glow hovered over her fingertips.

Melissa pulled her hands over her mouth and gasped. She didn't get up and run. She must have been too terrified to move.

"You have betrayed this coven," I told my father. "We could have protected her and found another way to find where Maurice was creating this potion and those who have betrayed our kind. You are a traitor and no longer my father. Get out of this house."

I couldn't stop those words, even if I wanted to. I had to protect our coven, and he couldn't be trusted. I ached at the thought of losing my dad, but we had no choice. It was up to us to get her back.

Roland gripped his phone and stormed out. He didn't even defend himself. When he reached the courtyard, he lifted his phone to his ear and spoke to someone on the other line and looked at me one last time before leaving the grounds.

Everyone lowered their powers, and I turned to Melissa. "I'm so sorry. I didn't know that was going to happen." I inched toward her.

She lifted her hands, putting her palms out in front of her to stop me from moving any closer. "I can't do this," she said, tears welling up in her eyes. She grabbed her purse from the back of her chair and ran out the door.

CHAPTER THIRTY FIVE

Mercy

"What time is your meeting?" I asked Maurice, who was adjusting the buckle to his suit pants. "You look sexy, by the way."

He smiled and leaned forward, kissing me passionately on the lips. "God, you're gorgeous." We released our kiss and I felt my cheeks grow red.

After he adjusted his tie, he grabbed his keys and wallet from the dresser and inched toward me again. "Two hours, but LA traffic is a nightmare, so I'm going to head out now." He leaned in again, kissed my neck, and dragged his lips under my ear, trailing his tongue up to my earlobe and nibbling slightly. "I'll miss you," he whispered.

I smiled back and bit my lower lip. "Not as much as I'll miss you."

After he left, I hurried to take a shower, taking my time as the warm water hit my skin. This week had been exciting but also exhausting. Julian had given me a tour of the city, and I'd spent most days and nights hanging out by the beach, and each night when I stood under the moonlight, I was drawn to the light that shined down on the ocean. It was as if the moon was pulling me in but was just out of reach.

Jade kept her distance from me. I wasn't sure what her problem was. It was as if she hated me, but I couldn't figure out why. She watched me sometimes from the other side of the room, and every time Maurice put his hands on me, she'd scrunch her nose and walk out of the room. Did she not want me to be happy, or were her feelings more personal when it came to Maurice? Had she loved him?

After a day at the beach, I met up with Julian for a smoothie on Main, and he took a call once we sat down at the outdoor tables.

"Yes, I have her," he told the caller on the other end, then paused. "Are you sure?" He pulled the phone away from his ear and muffled the bottom of his phone. "Will you be okay if I take you to Santa Monica with me? You can see the city on the drive and sit in the lobby while I take care of some business with Maurice."

This sounded exciting. I mean, not sitting in a lobby, but since I had been here, I hadn't been to any other city. Los Angeles was where Hollywood stars lived, and maybe they'd take me to go see the Hollywood sign.

"I'd love to!" I said with excitement.

"Okay, see you in about an hour or so," he said to the caller on the other end.

"Was that Maurice?"

He shook his head. "No."

That was all he said. There was no explanation, no telling me who it was. Just, "No."

We drove for over an hour, and I peered out the window, watching the cars zoom past us and cut each other off. We reached an industrial building near the Santa Monica pier. I entered, staggering behind him, and I eyed the receptionist smacking gum with a wide-open mouth, and she stood when we approached the counter.

"Julian, darling. It's nice to see you," she said, leaning in to kiss him on each cheek. She had a beautiful accent but I wasn't sure from where. She had short, blonde hair, blue eyes, freckles on her nose, and crooked teeth.

When he pulled away from her, Julian signaled for me to follow, but I stopped in front of her and held out my hand. "Hi, I'm Mercy."

She looked down at my hand and back at my face. She didn't shake my hand, didn't smile, but simply turned and walked back to her desk. I turned to Julian and shrugged my shoulders.

She was so rude.

He held out his hand. "Don't worry about her. Come."

I followed him down the hall, which was framed with glass windows, and through the glass, I saw beautiful purple plants growing inside a greenhouse. The plants lined several racks. Whatever they were growing, they needed plenty of it. We entered a spacious room with tall ceilings. The room was massive, but it wasn't the size that caught my attention, but the equipment inside.

"What is this place?" I asked.

"This is where we work. We've been developing Freedom Corporation for a year now, and we are about to launch our first product. We're still working out a few kinks and last-minute ingredients, but once we do—" He stopped as we both looked up at a large steel tank in front of us. "It will change their kind forever."

"Vampires?"

He nodded. "Yes. Vampires never had to seek out the ability to walk in the light because they depended on a witch to save them from that curse. But when they learned that was a lie, the vampire race joined forces with my coven to create a spell, a potion that, when given to a vampire, will enable them to walk in the light, forever. Not just a temporary solution like I've been able to provide."

I placed my hand on the cold steel of the tank and looked back at him. "How?"

This baffled me. From what I'd learned this last week, vampires were never able to walk in the light. Could it really work? Could Maurice finally join me on the beach during the day? That would be a dream.

"Dark magic. It's the only way, because witches are forbidden to help vampires. You were one of the smart ones, Mercy. You wanted to help. You knew there was good in them, and that's what made you fall in love with Maurice. You understood each other."

I blushed when he said, "fall in love." I surely felt a strong connection to him. Did I love him?

"We are just short a few ingredients, then we can start testing it on vampire subjects."

Test trials. But what if it didn't work? Would they die? No, Maurice wouldn't put his own kind in danger like that.

I looked around again. There were machines, tubes, and cases all over the place. On the righthand side sat a bunch of computers and technology that looked far too complicated for me to understand. Right as I approached the computers, Maurice walked in. "Mercy, glad you're here to see this."

He walked up, kissed me on the lips, and pulled back when I heard someone clear their throat. A woman with short black hair, and stunningly beautiful, stood behind Maurice with her arms crossed over her chest. "So, this is Mercy. How delightful it is to meet you. I'm Clara."

Would she reject me, too?

I held out my hand. "Hi. Nice to meet you, Clara."

She grabbed my hand and shook it with a firm grip. "Welcome to Freedom Corp." She let go and looked at Maurice with an odd grin. "I hope you like what we're doing here. It's been quite a year developing this potion, but once we're finished, we'll be able to help so many lives. Just think about it. This potion will create a barrier on vampires' skin to protect them from the UV rays that destroy them. Wouldn't that be amazing?"

I nodded. Why was she making me so nervous? "Yes . . . yes, it would," I said. Then, I looked at Maurice. "I'd love to see the rest."

Maurice smiled and brushed my hair over my ear. "I'd love to show you something, Mercy."

"Okay," I said as he led me out the door and down the hall. We entered another room, which had clear stalls toward the back, and . . . people were inside.

My stomach twisted. "Maurice, what the hell is this?"

He laughed. "Don't worry. Their sacrifice is going to save us."

"But they're prisoners. What are you doing, Maurice? This is wrong."

He laughed. "I don't care."

The room spun around me as my nerves took over. Did he want me to hate him? Why was he acting so cruel? Did I really date, maybe even love, someone like this? I wished so badly I could remember everything.

He gripped my arm and leaned down to whisper in my ear, "Do you have something you want to say to me?" My heart raced, and it nearly exploded in my chest. I couldn't speak. I just shook my head and looked down at my feet.

He let go of my wrist and walked over to Clara as she entered the room. "We have all five, now. Alexander came in last night," she said. The name sounded familiar. I walked closer to the clear stall and looked in. The first was a young girl, about my age. She was sitting with her knees to her chest, rocking back and forth. How long had she been in here?

I moved over to the next. A man in his forties stood in the corner, his arms folded. He looked straight at me, but his face was fierce, like he wanted to rip me to pieces. I wished I could tell him I had nothing to do with this. Next was an elderly woman. Her hair was silver, and she was curled up in the fetal position. I couldn't tell if she were sleeping, but she wouldn't look up, either. The fourth was a beautiful blonde woman, and she stood right at the front of the glass and stared at me. She put her hand up to the glass and tapped. She was saying something, but I couldn't hear. Her eyes grew wide as she threw her hands up and screamed at me while hitting the glass. I backed into Maurice. He wrapped his arms around me, pulling me further back.

"That is Abigail. She's a wild one, isn't she?" he asked.

I shook my head. "She's trying to tell me something."

He leaned down to my ear. "Would you like to see the last one?" The heat from his breath tickled my skin until each hair stood up on my neck. I didn't want to be here anymore, but I nodded anyway.

When we reached the fifth stall, I looked at a middle-aged man, handsome, with dark brown hair, and the look he gave me was pained. His eyes searched mine as if we were connected in some way. I placed my hand on the glass, and he put his hand flushed with mine on the other side.

"Who is this man?" I asked.

Maurice was now by my side, but this man behind the glass only held my gaze.

"His name is Alexander." He fisted my hair and pulled my head back. I winced. "We need their sacrifice to complete the spell. Then, we'll need you."

He released his grip, and I turned to him. "Me?"

He grabbed my right hand and traced my palm with his index finger. "We need your beautiful green light to activate the potion as the final touch. You'll be helping millions of vampires experience the freedom of the light."

I shook my head. "But I don't have any magic. You told me it had been taken from me."

Clara stood in front of me now. "Julian," she said. Julian was now next to me, grabbing my arm and pulling me into the last stall at the end. I tried to pry away his hands, which gripped on my arm, but he was too strong.

"Stop, Julian. Let me go. Stop!"

He slid open a glass door and threw me in.

No.

He shut the door and raised his hands over the glass in a circle, and black smoke trickled from his fingers. He swirled it around until the door sealed on the right side. I pulled at the door, but it wouldn't budge. I slammed my fist against it hard, but it wouldn't break.

No! I will not be kept in a cage.

What was happening?

CHAPTER THIRTY SIX

Mercy

I hopped up with a sudden urge to pee. There weren't any toilets in these tiny stalls. I banged on the door.

"Hello?"

But no one came. "I'm going to pee myself if you don't open this damn door."

Julian was in front of the glass and moved his hands in a circle again to unlock it. As soon as it opened, he grabbed my arm and escorted me to the bathroom. After I relieved myself, I took my time washing my hands.

I cannot go back in that stall.

Julian knocked on the door. "Hurry up."

I opened the door and flipped him off, moved past him, but he grabbed my arm again. "Watch it!"

Without thinking or caring about the consequences, I spit in his face. "Go to hell."

Maurice entered and let out what sounded like a hiss. "Enough. Don't put her back. We're ready for her."

Maurice grabbed me this time, and when I looked back at the glass stalls, they were empty.

We walked into the main room with the large tank and

standing on a platform were the other five that were kept as prisoners here. Their hands were tied behind their backs, and they looked as if they had been drugged.

"What is happening? What are you planning to do?"

He gestured to the people on the platform and said, "They're going to be our sacrifice." He turned and smiled. "The world is made up of five Universal Elements. Centuries ago, five families represented these elements. Other witches had to use spell books to harness those powers. But not those families. If that wasn't special enough, an angel came down and gave them each a child, their spirit being the Element itself. It allowed them to have a direct connection on this earth. Pretty powerful, don't you think?"

I didn't answer.

"These five are descendants from those families," Maurice said.

He moved over to the first, pulled out a knife, held it to her throat, and sliced it in one swift motion.

"Water," he said as her blood spilled from her wound. I yelped and covered my eyes.

He killed her. Oh, my God. He killed her!

"Hold her head up so she can watch," he commanded of Julian, who pulled at my hair and yanked my head up to stare in their direction. Maurice walked behind the man, who had been in the second stall and slit his throat, too. "Air." Then to the old woman. "Earth."

I let out a loud sob and gasped for air as anxiety filled my body. Once he reached the young blonde girl, I tried to step forward, but Julian yanked me back. "Please don't do this, Maurice."

The woman looked me straight in the eyes and called my name. "Mercy!"

She repeated my name, but the second time, she screamed it. Maurice slapped her hard across her face. "Shut up."

"Mercy, you need to use your powers. Use them now!" she said. Panic rose in my chest as he slit her throat.

"Stop! Please, Maurice."

Tears welled in my eyes.

This isn't happening.

"Fire," he said as her body collapsed to the floor.

The last one stood, keeping his eyes glued on mine. He must have been drugged as he rocked from side to side. I hoped the drugs they had given him would take away his pain. They were sick. All of them. They were sadistic, making me watch these senseless murders.

I thought about what the woman they had called Abigail had said to me. Use my powers? I didn't have any. Maybe I did, but I didn't know how to use them.

He held the knife under the last man's throat. They called him Alexander, and I felt like he was someone I knew. Someone I loved.

I stepped forward, but Julian pulled me back again.

"Say goodbye to your father, Mercy." He slit his throat and blood poured out of his neck. "Spirit."

My father?

I looked up in horror as Maurice stepped down from the platform. I watched their blood ooze out of their necks and flow to the center until their blood mixed together in a pile of misery and death.

Maurice gripped my hands and squeezed. "Focus, Mercy. We need you now."

He pulled my hands out, palms facing the five dead bodies in front of me. "Let me go!" I screamed.

"I need your power. Use it!" he yelled.

"I don't know how," I explained. "What's supposed to happen?"

Maurice gripped my waist and leaned in close to my ear. "I just killed your father. I've made you believe that you belonged to me. Tricked you into loving me. I kissed you. I even had your body, making you think that we were something special. How does that make you feel?"

Angry. That made me incredibly angry. It was all a lie. I knew I couldn't love someone like this, but I wasn't going to let my anger give them the power they needed. I wasn't going to let them use me this way.

Except, I felt something stirring inside just then. I felt these powers he had spoken of. They radiated through my body and reached my hands. I looked down and saw the light for the first time, but I wasn't going to give them my power that they needed. Instead, I flung my head back and head-butted Maurice so hard, I heard a crunch, then I ran. Julian grabbed the collar of my shirt and yanked me back. I pulled my hands forward and blasted him across the room as soon as he stood over me. Once I reached the door, Clara was standing in front of it. I lifted my hands to blast her, but the moment the power landed in front of her, she caught it in her hand and threw my magic toward the bodies on the floor.

No!

I backed up into a body, and a needle pricked my neck.

They pulled me toward the platform, and I watched in horror as my power, which she had directed their way, swirled in circles, with the blood of their victims circling around like a tornado until it was mixed together as one.

Clara walked up to the platform and moved her hands from side to side, directing the liquid up to the large tank in the center of the room, and lowered it inside.

She was a witch, and that scared me more than being around Maurice. She just took my own powers and used them against me.

She smiled and stepped toward me, but I couldn't attack anymore. The drugs they'd given me had taken over.

And I shut my eyes.

CHAPTER THIRTY SEVEN

Mercy

When my eyes opened, I was chained to my bed at my wrists and ankles.

Oh, come on!

I looked at the door, which was open, and called out, "Maurice!" But he didn't come.

I huffed, laying my head back down and closing my eyes. I focused on the power that radiated from my palms.

Did he really think I wouldn't try this?

The powers hovered over the chains, and I focused, hoping it would penetrate the metal, but nothing happened.

"Hello, Mercy," Jade said as she walked in. "I'm not supposed to take those off, so I have to feed you and give you the drugs that are keeping your powers stabilized." Her voice was sluggish, as if I were a huge inconvenience to her.

She carried a tray of food and a glass of orange juice. She set the tray down on the nightstand and stuck a straw in the drink. "Here."

"No, thank you," I said, turning my head away from her. "It could be poisoned."

She laughed. "Ha! Not like it would kill you. Drink it. You're going to dehydrate."

"Then, give me water," I snapped, turning back to her.

Her face hardened. "Look, you stubborn little witch. Drink and eat what I give you, and I'll leave. If you don't, he will punish me."

I laughed. "Good."

Her fangs appeared, and she lurched toward me but stopped before she reached my neck. Her breath was heavy against my skin. She was so close, but she wouldn't bite down.

Why? She's a vampire, that's what they do.

She let out a frustrated growl, grabbed the tray, and stormed out.

She left me alone again, which I was both thankful for and worried about. How long were they going to chain me up like this? What if I had to pee?

The clock on the nightstand read ten in the morning, and when I looked back at the ceiling above me, the door opened again. This time, it was Maurice.

"I'm heading back to the lab today to start preparing the vials of potion you helped us make last night. Thank you, by the way. After last year, learning about what you did, I found you worthless, but really, you were the key to helping us after all, just in a different way."

He rubbed the back of his fingers against my cheek and my skin crawled. "What are you talking about?"

His devilish smile grew wide. "You and I, Mercy, have

done this before, but in a different setting and circumstance." He kept stroking my cheeks, and it was pissing me off.

"I've never loved you, have I? It was a lie from the start."

He removed his hand finally, and I hadn't realized that I was tensing up the entire time. I relaxed my shoulders into the mattress. "We were never in love, but I wanted you then, and I still want you now."

"Oh, please. You want to use my powers. That's it."

His face grew fierce and he brought his hand to my throat, squeezing hard. "I already got what I wanted. I could let you go back to your coven, but you're too dangerous with them, and with the help of Julian removing all the negative feelings and memories you have of me, you and I could have a future together. It's a shame you can't die, or I would turn you into a vampire. Maybe then you'd see that a powerful man needs a powerful woman."

"I'd rather choke on my own vomit," I spat out. As I turned to look away from him, his fingers lifted from my throat.

I didn't want to see the look on his face, but I could only imagine. "Eat when Jade brings you food!" His voice was harsh and authoritative.

I didn't watch him leave, but I heard the door shut.

I think I laid there for over three hours or so.

Waiting.

Bored.

Thirsty.

The door creaked open again, and I thought it was Maurice coming back, but it was Jade. She didn't have food this time, but she was carrying a bottle of water. "Open," she instructed. And I did. I can't remember the last time I had been so thirsty.

After I drank the entire bottle, she undid my chains with a key and stepped back. I rubbed my wrist.

My brows furrowed. "Why couldn't I break the chains with my magic?"

"Julian put a spell on it, but I'm still able to open with the key. Use the bathroom," she commanded. I hurried to the bathroom quickly and relieved myself, as she sat on the bed, waiting.

I could have taken her out right then and there if I wanted to. Just a flick of my wrist and I could have shot my powers out toward her and ran.

I wasn't sure if anyone else was in the house, but I had to at least try to escape.

"If you're thinking of hurting me, please don't," she said as I entered back into the room.

I slowly walked toward her. "Are you going to tie me back up?"

She shook her head. "Come. Follow me to the library."

I didn't understand what was happening. She seemed

like she didn't hate me in that moment. She was being . . . nice.

I followed her to the library, which I had only been in a few times. Her coffee mug sat on a small table, and next to it was the play *Romeo and Juliet*.

I snickered.

"What's so damn funny?" she asked.

"I don't know, Jade. You seem like you'd be reading something darker. Like *Dracula* or *Salem's Lot*."

She snickered this time, picking up her book. "Yeah, I don't come off as the romantic type, do I?"

I shrugged. "Well, there is tragedy in that story, isn't there?"

She smiled, set the book back down, and strode toward me. "I love him, you know?"

I knew who she was talking about. It wasn't Julian. It was Maurice. "Did you date?"

She nodded. "A long time ago. Now, I work for him."

I looked down, gathering up my thoughts. "He's my worst enemy, isn't he?"

She nodded. "Yes, but he's obsessed with you."

My stomach twisted into knots at those words. Love wasn't scary. Hatred wasn't even scary. Both love and hate allowed you to feel free. But obsession. That was something you'd have to escape from.

"What am I?" I asked her.

She turned, and her lips made a straight line. "You're *our* worst enemy."

She walked over to the bookshelf, pulled out a book, and opened it. It wasn't a book, though. It was a box with a small cut out. She pulled out a large key and walked up to me.

"What does that open?" I asked.

She placed it in my hand. "The other answer to your question."

I looked down at the key, then eyed the hallway connected to the library. The hallway led to that thick door I was forbidden to open.

"I'll be in my room for a while," she said.

I nodded my head, and she walked down the hall toward the stairs which led to the second level, and I walked to that door. I slipped the key in and it unlocked. It worked on all the locks. I turned the wheel, and it opened the door.

It wasn't a safe. The only thing in the there was a coffin, which stood at the center of the room.

I walked slowly to the coffin, placed my hands on the lid, and lifted it. There was a handsome man inside. He looked dead, but no different from Jade or Maurice.

I placed my hand on his chest, and I felt it rise. He was alive, or, undead.

A vampire.

He looked so familiar to me. I pulled my hands up to his face and closed my eyes. I didn't know what was wrong, so I didn't know how I could help this man, but I allowed my powers to come through me and into him. After a few moments, his eyes opened, and he looked right at me.

"Mercy, you're okay." He sat up and reached for me, but I stepped back, almost stumbling over my feet.

"Who . . . who are you? Do I know you?" My voice trembled.

His eyes were glistening, and his tortured stare answered my questions. I was someone he cared about.

I must know and care for him.

He climbed out of the coffin and walked toward me, holding up his hands. "I won't hurt you."

This time, when he reached for me, I didn't move back. Instead, I stepped toward him, touching his icy cold fingers. "My name is Dorian. And we were in love centuries ago. All I remember is Maurice telling me that he needed me as leverage if you refused to cooperate. It was a witch that put me under a spell in here. You can't trust them."

"I know. I don't remember who I was, but I know all of this was a lie."

Dorian's eyes looked heavy, and he didn't look well. "You look sick," I said to him.

"I need to feed."

"So, you're a vampire, then?"

He nodded.

"Here." I pulled my hair to the side, not even hesitating to help him. "Please, it's okay. Drink."

He shook his head. "I can't. Not your blood. I need to be able to use my vampire strength to help you."

I creased my brow. "I don't understand."

His eyes stared into mine. He inched closer, and for a

moment, I hesitated, started to step back, but I stopped. He leaned in and placed his lips to mine and deepened the kiss.

The fire that burned inside me leaped to the surface, aching for more of his touch. His taste was familiar, his touch was a memory. My mind was in the moment, then it wasn't. I remembered the first time our lips touched, but it was a different life. We were different. It was long ago.

Dorian! I remembered him.

Julian did this.

I saw it happen. Julian had placed his hands over my temples outside of Dorian's car. I grabbed at his wrist and tried to use my powers, but it happened so fast. He pulled at my hair and yanked me down until my knees crushed into the pavement on the side of the road. Dorian had screamed for me in the distance.

When I came to, I looked at Dorian and smiled with relief. I was back. I remembered everything.

"You remember?"

I nodded. "I remember."

He grabbed my hand as we heard the floorboard creek outside the room. "You have ten minutes to get as far away from here as possible," Jade said. "Julian is on his way back."

"We have to go, Mercy. Now!"

"Wait," Jade said.

"What is it?" I asked.

"It's daylight. He can't leave."

I looked at Dorian and my eyes widened. "You must turn back. You must, Dorian."

He shook his head.

"You don't have a choice. You're going to be dead when he gets here. You can't help me fight if you're dead," I said as panic rose in my chest.

He hesitated but grabbed my hand. "Okay."

I felt the pounding of my heart against my chest as I held my wrist up to his lips. Then he bit down.

I closed my eyes, feeling the blood drain from my veins and enter his mouth. The feeling of euphoria took over, and when I opened my eyes, tears welled in his.

I placed my hand on his cheek, feeling the warmth as his skin came back to life.

"You don't have time to have a moment, you two. Go," Jade said.

When we reached the door, I turned to Jade. "He's going to kill you for helping us."

"I know, and I don't care."

No. This wasn't right. "I can turn you back, too. Right now. You can come with us. You don't deserve this."

She laughed. "Yes, I do. I've done disturbing things, Mercy. I deserve to die for what I've done. He doesn't love me, and he was the only reason I allowed myself to stay alive all these years. I don't want to be a vampire, but I also don't want to be human because I know that the moment my soul returns, I will be haunted by the guilt of everything I have done. I'm ready to die."

I turned to Dorian and shook my head. "No!" I turned back to her. "No!"

"We have to go, Mercy."

"I can't leave," I said. "Jade, please. Let me turn you."

She shook her head, a tear running down her face. "Get out of here. Now, or I'll put you both in that coffin."

Dorian grabbed my wrist, yanking me out of the house, me resisting him the whole way. I'll force her if I must. She wasn't going to sacrifice herself like that. I didn't know why I cared so much, but I did. Nothing about this was right. Maurice would not be the cause of her life being taken from this earth.

I yanked free from his grip, running back to the house, but she was already on the porch, the sun beating down onto her pale white skin. The sun would be the weapon to take her life.

"No!" I screamed as I watched her body burst into flames. It didn't last long. Not for a vampire. She was ash before she could scream.

I fell to my knees. I had never seen a vampire die by the sun before. It was always so quick, with a flick of my wrist while I gripped to a stake. This was something else. This wasn't a sight I was prepared for.

"Now, Mercy. We have to go now."

I felt his hands on mine again, pulling me away from that prison we were held in. A prison that, moments ago, I believed to be my home. I believed it to be the place I shared with a man I loved. A lie. A fantasy created by a demented narcissist. He wouldn't win today. Not with me. Not with Dorian. And not with Jade.

We took off down the road. We had no money, no phone. I had no idea where we were going to go.

We hurried down to the beach, and I spotted a couple sitting on the sand. "Excuse me. We have an emergency. Can I please use your phone? I have no money to give you. I'm sorry."

The man shook his head, put his arms around the woman, and walked away.

Okay, I get it. We're strangers. Not everyone will be that skeptical, though.

I pointed to a teenager. "There."

This time, Dorian spoke. "Excuse me, we have an emergency. Can we borrow your phone for just one minute?"

She nodded and smiled. "Um . . . sure, here."

"Thank you," I said, grabbed the phone, and dialed Joel's number, and he picked up right away. "Hello?"

"Joel, it's Mercy," I said, relieved to hear his voice.

"Mercy!" he said in reply. "You guys! It's Mercy on the phone." I heard shouts and commotion in the background.

"Who's there?"

"Lily and Bradley came over tonight. Oh, Mercy, we've been so worried."

"Look, we don't have a lot of time. We're on the north side of the Huntington Beach Pier. We need you to teleport us home."

"Give me five minutes. I need to grab a map to pinpoint the exact location."

"Okay, see you soon."

I hung up the phone and handed it back to the girl. "Thank you again."

The girl continued down to the pier and we were alone again, and that was a relief as the portal was about to open.

A few minutes later, the entrance to the vortex opened, and we stepped inside the portal. It zipped us through faster than it took for us to blink.

We landed in the front living room, but no one was there. "Joel? Lily?" I called.

"I'll check the kitchen," I said.

Dorian eyed the back door. "I'll check out back."

We split up, and I called for them again but heard nothing. I looked for Dorian near the back door, but I didn't see him, so I walked out to the backyard.

"Dorian?" I called.

I then spotted the backside of . . .

"Bradley?" He turned around, holding the carved-out end of our missing dagger.

I stared at him, confusion clouded my senses and my heart pounding hard against my chest. "You guys found the dagger?" My question was stupid. No, that's not what this was. Especially after seeing the face Bradley was giving me.

His face read hatred and disgust.

"Where is everyone?" I asked. He gestured with his other hand to the right. Sitting under their willow tree were three bodies, sprawled out. I could see their chests rising and falling. They weren't dead.

I looked back at Bradley. "What did you do to them? Why are you doing this? Who are you?"

My questions came out fast, one after another, without skipping a beat. I didn't understand any of this, but I was ready to kill this asshole as soon as I had answers.

"I really didn't think we'd ever see you again, but I'm glad I've kept the dagger with me everywhere I went, just in case," he said, snickering. "What a great opportunity to catch you off guard, once you came through that portal." He spoke in an accent I hadn't heard coming from his mouth before. He was British, and before I could speak again, he continued. "You're just as stupid and careless as your father."

What? This is about my dad?

"You knew my father?"

He pulled his glasses off, and tossed them on the yard. His face was hard and furious. "Your father killed my wife."

I was stunned silent for a minute. I remembered my father's story about the woman he had accidentally killed. He wasn't able to stop before he took too much of her blood. He escaped before the husband came back, but he watched the man through the bedroom window, holding his wife until she slipped away in his arms.

"I'm sorry about your wife, Bradley, but what does that have to do with me? Your quarrel is with my father, and he died yesterday. Maurice killed him right in front of me."

I understood the need for revenge, but no one would go through this much trouble for revenge. Why kill innocent people? For one person?

All of this. All of the death couldn't be because my father killed his wife, unless it screwed up his head so badly, he was acting without any remorse.

He stepped toward me, and I raised my hands, ready to use my powers.

"Ah. Ah. I wouldn't do that if I were you," he warned. Then, he gestured toward Dorian and my family, laying on the ground. "There is magic connecting me to them. If you kill me, they'll die in less than a minute."

"How?" I asked, my voice steady. Finally gaining composure.

"Ha! I'm not going to tell you how the spell works, my dear."

I cringed at the sound of him calling me "dear."

"No, how did you do it? The killings? Was there a vampire doing your dirty work?"

He stepped toward me, and I moved back. "No. That was all me." He pulled something out of his pocket and held it up, smiling. A proud grin pulled at his lips. "I designed this after I mastered my plan to draw you out. How to entice you to kill your own father."

I narrowed my eyes in on an object that looked like vampire fangs. Two prongs, a little over an inch apart from each other, connected by black rope or string.

"It makes the perfect bite mark into one's neck."

He was crazy. And I was pissed. His need for revenge was so powerful, he had taken innocent lives.

"But they were innocent, Bradley. You killed humans.

People who had families who cared about them. Have you no shame for what you've done? All for what? So that I'd think it was my father and kill him to avenge your wife?"

He placed the fang device back into his pocket, and I could see him gripping the dagger tightly in his other palm. "No one is innocent, especially not you. After you turned your father back into a human, I knew I couldn't continue with the original plan. But me killing his daughter? Now, that's rich. The perfect revenge. An eye for an eye. You're the one person he loved on this earth." He stepped closer, but when I moved back, my backside hit a patio post. "I was hesitant at first, because we witches would be without Spirit again, but then I thought about it." He tapped the dagger on his thigh, just as I had seen Kylan do at the cove a year ago. "Would the powers really leave this earth if a witch kills them? If I killed your coven, then I would gain your powers, right? You kill a witch, you get their power."

"I don't think it works like that with the Chosen Ones, Bradley."

"Your mother thought so, didn't she? Isn't that why she tried to kill you?"

He was right. It wasn't a scenario that had really crossed our minds since this all started. We were so worried about vampires coming after us, we didn't think about the fact that other witches could also want us dead in order to take our power.

"It doesn't matter," I said. "You'd have to get close enough to me first." I held up my hands, ready to fight him. But I couldn't kill him until the spell on my family was released. I had to disempower him somehow.

Before he took a step closer, I released my energy, blasting him up into the air and flying him back toward the back fence. Once he hit, the dagger flew from his hands.

I dashed for it.

I didn't get far. He had my legs pinned to the ground and yanked me closer to him. I punched him hard in his face, but he barely flinched. He grabbed my head, and I felt dizziness take over. The power he had was something I hadn't encountered before from other witches. He created a sense of vertigo in my head, and I was on the verge of throwing up, but I kept my hands steady as I released more of my powers. I tried to summon the earth around me, the dirt, the trees, the air, fire, but nothing worked. I couldn't focus enough with the pounding going on in my head to conjure up my magic. He was crippling me as if I had overdosed on drugs.

"Stop it, Bradley. You don't want to do this. My powers will kill you if you take them. You can't handle this amount of power."

He just laughed at me, while continuing to distort my mind.

My pleading was pointless, but I had to try something. I brought my knee up and kicked him in the groin, causing him to fall to his side. I was on my feet before he could grab me, and I side kicked him, causing him to fly through the air and slam into a tree.

I blasted my powers toward him, and it kept him pinned

to the ground. I gripped his throat and threw a punch, but when his hands lifted, he shot back powers I hadn't seen coming, and I flew through the air, landing on my back.

Just as I looked up, I saw Bradley's face in doubles, triples, a blur of confusion. He was now on top of me, pressing his hand to my head, causing an extreme amount of vertigo, and I could no longer use my powers on him. I tried to lift my fist, but I missed his body, and he gripped my arm, pulling it back down.

Once my hand was free to strike again, I mustered up every ounce of power I had in my body. Not from my magic, but from my own physical strength. I lifted it up, slowly brought it back down to my body, and thrusted my fist forward with every ounce of strength that I had in me until my fist broke through his chest.

I felt the crushing of his skin, his muscles, his sternum, and grabbed his heart firmly. I held on, his eyes wide open, blood pouring from his mouth, but before I yanked his heart from his chest, the piercing sound of a dagger plunged into my stomach.

With the dagger still in me, I squeezed his heart with my hand, and yanked it out of his chest.

Bradley fell over my body, which caused him to push the dagger deeper into my belly, but I was able to push him off so I could sit up, but barely. Blood spewed out of my mouth, and I felt like I was choking.

I eyed my family and Dorian and moved as fast as I could, though my body was weakening by the second. I covered each body with my hands, bringing them back from the brink of death. They'd all started to fade away after I ripped Bradley's heart from his chest.

I watched all three of their chests rise and fall. They were alive. I sighed with heavy relief, but I couldn't hold on anymore. The power from the dagger was taking my life.

I was going to die.

"Mercy!" Dorian cried as I fell in his arms. My name was the last thing I heard before I slipped away.

CHAPTER THIRTY EIGHT

Mercy

I looked down a long hallway where the walls were bright white. Was this heaven?

I continued down the hallway until I reached a door, but when I placed my hand on the knob, my hand went through it and I stepped onto dark pavement. The air was thick, and the only things I saw in front of me were bodies walking shoulder to shoulder like a crowded street in a city. Most of the people walking looked lost, sad, or scared.

No, this wasn't heaven.

"Excuse me," I said to a young woman with golden blonde hair. She stopped and turned to me, her eyes widened, and her face looked terrified.

"It's you. That means . . ."

I died. She meant to say that I had died.

I nodded. "I think so. What is this place?"

She looked around as people passed by, ignoring us. "This is the underworld. It's a place where the spirits go when their bodies are still connected to the earth in some way. I'm a vampire down there. You were here not so long ago."

I thought about her words. Vampires were undead, but their souls were taken from them when they were turned. Was this the place where they'd go?

"We can't move on until our bodies on earth die, or you help us come back using your blood. We've all hoped you'd save us; bring us back to our bodies and our consciousness. But now you're here. Which means we're doomed."

I looked around again at the people walking around in their lost state and asked, "What did you mean by me being here before?"

"Of course you don't remember. After they hung you at the Gallows, you came here. You're bound to your coven, so your spirit doesn't truly move on unless they all do."

I thought about how Caleb had finally found a way to bring me back nineteen years ago, and how difficult it must have been for him to find my soul. It could only be done by a special kind of magic. It was a magic that could have only been done once.

Was I doomed to be in this place forever? If I were truly bound to the earth, and now my body was dead again, what was going to happen to me? What about these souls that were stuck here?

"I'm sorry. I tried. I tried and I failed," I told her.

She smiled for the first time since I'd stopped her. "You can still watch over them."

"How?" I asked.

She smiled one last time and faded into the crowd, without answering me. I now stood alone.

I knelt on a grassy lawn near a tree. When I looked ahead through the crowd of people in front of me, I could see through them like a window had been opened for me to look through. There lay my body in Joel's backyard, with Dorian holding me in his arms. And he was weeping.

I wished they could hear or see me so I could comfort them in their pain. Lily buried her face in Joel's chest, sobbing over the loss of her niece.

I really was gone.

CHAPTER THIRTY NINE

Caleb

"No!" I gasped. Every part of my being prayed I didn't just feel that. I eyed the coven and their eyes grew wide.

"Oh, my God!" Leah screamed. She held her chest and we all screamed out in agony, feeling a deep sense of sorrow and pain we hadn't experienced since the Witch Trials.

We felt it. We felt her die.

"Let's go. We need to move. Now," I yelled to the coven as we filed outside and into Leah's car.

Joel had just texted me that he was teleporting Mercy and Dorian to his home after they escaped. But moments after, we felt her life taken from us. Had something gone wrong inside the portal?

I drove as fast as I could, not caring if a cop tried to pull us over. Not caring about the hundreds of laws that I was breaking to get there.

"Caleb, she's already gone. Slow down before you kill someone," Ezra said.

I ignored him. I had to get there.

We pulled into the driveway, jumped out, and hurried

inside. We didn't see anyone in the kitchen, or even the family room. "Joel?" I yelled. The voice that followed wasn't his. It was Lily's.

"Caleb, come quickly."

Once we entered the backyard, the first body I saw was Bradley, laying lifeless on the floor with a hole in his chest, his motionless heart on the ground beside him. I cringed, but my attention immediately pulled to Lily sobbing under a willow tree. She and Joel held each other tightly. They knelt next to Dorian, whose back was facing us. When we walked around to face him, he held Mercy's lifeless and bloodied body in his arms. Lily held onto the dagger tightly in her hand. She placed it on the ground when we ran over to her.

"No!" I screamed, kneeling beside them, the coven following behind me.

I felt numb. We couldn't lose her again.

We all held hands, sobbing and shaking, our hearts aching over her loss. Not again.

I leaned down and kissed her on the forehead. "I'm so sorry, Mercy. I am so, so sorry." I leaned back. Everyone kissed her head and we sat in near silence. The only sounds were those of agony-filled weeping.

I looked up at the coven. "We're bringing her back." I didn't even think about my words. I knew what we had to do, but I had to convince the other three it was our duty to do it. We had to.

"We can't, Caleb," Ezra said. "The spell won't work again, but we can keep looking until we find another way."

I shook my head. "There is another way."

Their eyes met mine, and I knew they were confused. I was the only one who knew another way to bring her back. When I had found the spell to resurrect her eighteen years ago, the Shaman who helped make the spell had used the last remaining bark of the original tree on Gallows Hill. The same tree that took the lives of our fellow Salem witches centuries ago. Once it was gone, there'd be no more left. But he explained something else to me. He explained that if this were to happen again, a sacrifice would need to be made. It was the only way to give her enough power and magic to bring her back.

"Leah, Ezra, Simon," I said, pausing for a moment to gather the words. "Our powers are the only thing that can bring her back."

Leah lowered her brow. "Then we join hands and conjure whatever spell we have to in order to share our powers with her. Just tell us the spell, and we'll do it."

I shook my head. "Sharing our powers won't be enough."

Simon looked up, his eyes widening. He understood.

He turned to Leah. "We have to give up our elements."

Leah's breathing picked up pace. "If we give up our elements, we die."

I nodded slowly, and she nodded back in understanding.

"Well, we've lived a long life. I think I've done everything on my bucket list," Ezra said. We chuckled quietly to ourselves, everyone shedding a tear at the realization that we were all on the same page. Spirit couldn't be taken from the earth again, and Mercy was the only one strong enough to hold on to all five elements.

"Okay," Leah said, nodding again and wiping her eyes.

Simon gripped Leah's hand, and Ezra grabbed mine.

Lily and Joel stood and we embraced them and said our goodbyes. Lily leaned toward me. "We will find a way to make this right somehow."

I squeezed her hand, and the four of us gathered around Mercy's body. Dorian laid her down gently. He had been quiet the entire time as tears rolled down his face. Before he stood, he leaned closer to me and said, "Thank you."

He stood back with the others while Leah, Simon, and Ezra knelt with me. All four of us gripped our hands together in a circle, and I chanted the spell the witch doctor had taught me years ago. They mimicked the chant, and I felt my power as it radiated inside of me. It was more powerful than I had ever felt.

We stopped chanting, and Leah lifted her hands above her head. "I am Water. I give you my power."

Simon followed her lead. "I am Air. I give you my power."

"I am Earth. I give you my power," Ezra said.

Finally, I spoke my last words. "I am Fire. I give you my power."

As soon as the last word left my lips, we all collapsed to the ground.

CHAPTER FORTY

Mercy

My eyes opened and I looked at the grey clouds forming above. My eyes watered, and I rubbed the tears away before I sat up and saw my coven laying down on their backs, circling me on the grass.

I had seen everything. I saw what they did for me, and there wasn't anything I could do about it. They couldn't see me or hear me scream for them to stop. I couldn't get them to stop.

I felt the warmth of Fire, the flow of Water, the comfort of Earth, and the fresh breath of Air within me, circling my soul. They circled Spirit as if the five of us were one. My body didn't just conjure the power, it *was* the power. All five elements were inside me.

Their vessels, the bodies that walked with them, lay dead, but were they really dead if the elements that gave each one life to begin with were still empowered and thriving?

I looked to my right, and Dorian knelt with me. He reached out his hand, and I clasped it in mine.

Caleb's body was a few feet from where I knelt, and I inched toward him, dragging my knees against the prickly grass. After I placed the back of my fingers to his cheek, caressing his skin, I looked at the others.

"Joel?" I said. He had stood silently by the tree, holding on to Lily, waiting for me to speak. His and Lily's eyes were puffy and red from crying when they had thought I was gone forever.

This wasn't a moment to embrace each other and celebrate because I was alive.

No.

An evil man lay dead behind us with his heart ripped out. A man Lily loved, and she now knew he had lied to her to get to me.

Four of my friends, my family, my coven, lay dead before us. They had sacrificed themselves for me. There was nothing to rejoice in this moment.

Joel was now by my side, and Dorian moved over, allowing Joel to bring me to my feet. "We need to find four coffins," I said. "The three of us will perform a spell that will preserve their bodies until the day I find a way to bring them back."

Joel nodded. "My spell book has one, but it's dark, Mercy. It's dark magic, and I've never performed it before. The spell will last as long as their spirit is tied to the earth."

"Then we do it," I said.

I didn't care that it was dark magic. They were not leaving me.

"We'll keep the coffins locked in our family's mausoleum on 34th Street in Salem," I said. "We'll do it tonight before their bodies decompose."

Lily sauntered toward me and brought me in for a hug. I squeezed her tightly in my arms while the tears I held back now fell freely down my face.

"You're alive. I know that doesn't mean anything to you right now, but it does to me. I couldn't lose you, too," Lily said as she released me and turned to face Joel. "We need to do the spell now. I'll help you gather what's needed."

Lily and Joel went into his house, and I turned to face Dorian, who was now by my side.

"It's gone," I said, pointing to my chest.

He tilted his head slightly. "What's gone?"

"The spell. When I died, the spell died with me."

It took him a second to realize what I was saying. Then, his eyes grew wide. "How do you feel?" A faint smile pulled at his lips.

I walked closer to him and brought my hands to his cheeks, caressing his jawline with my fingers. A tear rolled down my face, and he wiped it with his hand.

I trailed my fingers down to his neck, gripping the hair on the back of his head and pulling him closer to me until our lips touched. He gently placed his hands on each side of my face, pulling us deeper into our kiss. The kiss was passionate, loving, and filled with centuries of undying love. The feeling in my heart showed me that I could never take it away again.

I wanted to embrace the emotions my body was screaming for, but my heart also ached for the loss of my family and a man I, too, had loved.

I would search for a way to bring my coven back, and I would continue the mission to save this world from creatures like Maurice. He was still out there. Kylan's spirit was still out there, also, and lives would be lost as long as they walked this earth.

But in *this* moment, it was just us.

Me and Dorian.

And I was in love with him.

EPILOGUE

Maurice

I looked down at a pile of ash at my doorstep and shrugged.

Jade.

A slight panic rose in my chest, followed by anger. Would Jade be so stupid to have let Mercy go?

I turned toward the limo outside my home and held up my finger, signaling to Clara that I would be a minute. I couldn't see her through the tinted windows, but I assumed she had seen me, knowing that crazy bitch was always watching my and everyone else's every move.

I walked into my house and sniffed. Not like it would have mattered. Mercy was still under that infuriating spell her uncle had cast upon her to mask her intoxicating scent.

I walked down the hall and stopped dead in my tracks when I saw the safe's door standing wide open.

My nostrils flared.

Where the hell is Julian?

When I neared my bedroom where we were keeping Mercy, I saw that Mercy was, indeed, gone. Her unlocked chains lie on the bed, and the syringe filled with the drugs I'd had Jade administer to her was full.

If Jade weren't already dead, I'd kill her.

I balled my hand into a fist, feeling the pressure build around my eyes, and my fangs protruded. I hissed as Clara walked into the bedroom.

"While you were playing house with her, she should have been locked up in a cage," she said in a huff. "Doesn't matter anymore. We got what we needed from her."

"*You* got what you needed from her." My jaw tightened. "I wasn't done with her. Not by a long shot."

Clara walked past me and picked up the syringe. "You really are a sadistic son of a bitch." She squeezed the syringe and emptied its liquid contents onto the floor. "But we have more pressing matters to address." She tossed the syringe into the trashcan in the corner of the room.

I followed her, and as we neared the front door, Julian entered the foyer. "She's at the factory. We have her bound in stall number five."

"Good," Clara said. "Vampire trials for the potion will start tomorrow. Our test subjects are going to be brought to the office at seven in the morning." She turned to Julian. "Maurice is in charge, and you'll obey him from now on. Once the subjects are brought in, we will proceed with the ceremony. Be there at nine," Clara ordered. "Oh, and Maurice?" She turned back to me.

I looked to her and waited for her order.

"I expect a proper goodbye before Kylan leaves Cami's body and takes over mine."

ACKNOWLEDGMENTS

Thank you to all my beta readers, editor, book cover designer, and the support from everyone who read book one, so I could make book two possible. I also want to give a special thank you to my family, who supported me throughout my writing journey.

There will be a book three coming out within the next year, which will conclude The Chosen Coven series.

ABOUT THE AUTHOR

D.L. Blade grew up in California and studied at the California Healing Arts College, going on to work as a massage therapist for thirteen years. D.L. now lives in Colorado, where she worked as a real estate agent for a time before deciding to concentrate on her family and her writing.

D.L. always loved writing, concentrating on poetry, rather than prose, when she was younger. That changed, however, when she had a dream one night and decided to write a book about it. In her spare time, D.L. enjoys a wide variety of hobbies, including reading, writing, attending rock concerts, and spending time outdoors with her family, camping, and going on outings.

In the future, D.L. hopes she can continue to write

exciting novels that will captivate her readers and bring them into the worlds she creates with her imagination.

Made in the USA
San Bernardino, CA
24 April 2020